Time flies. . . .

"Oh, this is awful!" Bess said. "Who would want to steal the library clock? I mean, who would have the heart?"

Ahead of us we saw Mrs. Corning at the circulation desk. She was literally pulling out her hair. Her normally perfect bun looked like a seeding dandelion, hairs drifting everywhere. She was also gesturing wildly at one of Chief McGinnis's officers.

"Mrs. Corning!" I shouted to her, momentarily forgetting that we were in a library and that I wasn't supposed to make a lot of noise.

Mrs. Corning looked in our direction. "Oh, Nancy, Nancy, Nancy!" she cried. "I'm so glad you're finally here!" She turned back to the officer. "Now, perhaps we'll be able to solve this crime!" she added in a hostile voice.

NANCY DREW
girl detective™

Available from Aladdin Paperbacks

NANCY DREW
DREW
girl detective ™

#12

Stop the Clock

CAROLYN KEENE

Aladdin Paperbacks
New York   London   Toronto   Sydney

First Aladdin Paperbacks edition July 2005

Copyright © 2005 by Simon & Schuster, Inc.

ALADDIN PAPERBACKS
An imprint of Simon & Schuster Children's Publishing Division
1230 Avenue of the Americas, New York, NY 10020

Manufactured in the United States of America
10   9   8   7

NANCY DREW is a registered trademark of
Simon & Schuster, Inc.

ALADDIN PAPERBACKS, NANCY DREW: GIRL DETECTIVE, and colophon are trademarks of Simon & Schuster, Inc.

Library of Congress Control Number 2004113787

ISBN-13: 978-0-689-87336-2   ISBN-10: 0-689-87336-0

Contents

Stop the Clock

Stolen!

"**W**atch out, Nancy!" **Bess** shouted.

I slammed on the brakes of my car just in time to miss an SUV speeding down Bluff Street. "Oops!"

"I'm telling you, Nancy," George said. "You've got to stay focused!"

"Sorry," I said. "I was just thinking about the library celebration and how we should decorate for it."

Actually George was right. I did need to stay more focused. The problem is, I usually have so much on my mind that it's racing a hundred miles per hour. It's pretty hard to stay focused with that kind of a brain.

Let me fill you in. We were headed to the Mahoney Library—a private library started as a pet project by the mother-in-law of the current Mrs. Mahoney, who is the wealthiest person in River Heights. In just a couple of weeks the library would be celebrating its seventy-fifth anniversary—and I was really excited because I had been recruited as a volunteer to help plan the festivities.

Frances Corning, the head librarian and the mother of a friend of mine, Helen Corning, had asked me to chair the decoration committee. The focus of the whole event would be the old clock. It was donated many years ago to the library by a local River Heights jeweler, Ben Mullins. It is *so* cool too. The face of the clock has large Roman numerals and is set inside a gold base. In each corner Mr. Mullins etched the face of a person famous in the history of River Heights. He never told anyone who the four people were, though—so people just keep guessing. It's kind of funny. Everyone in town is *sure* it's their relative's face on the clock.

"Nancy!" George shouted. "The light's still red!"

"I know, I know," I said. "I was planning to stop."

"It's usually not a good idea to stop in the *middle* of the intersection, Nancy," Bess said. "It makes it hard for cars to go through."

As you can see, George and Bess like to tease me, but I couldn't ask for better friends. Both of them help me so much on my cases, even if they get in the way sometimes. Take Bess, for starters. For her, every

2

crook has a very good reason for committing his or her crime. Bess just doesn't want to believe that people really do bad things. And sometimes, well . . . they do.

With George, I can never get through the mall without a trip to all the electronic stores. As if that wasn't bad enough, she feels that she has to explain in intricate detail how everything works. She knows more than most of the people who work there. Of course, that also means George is able to help her mother with her catering business. She can find anything and everything on the Internet.

I turned a corner and merged into traffic. "This morning I was thinking about all the stories I remember people telling about the library clock," I said. "It's really been a big part of the lives of a lot of people in River Heights."

"Yeah. Didn't you meet Ned under the clock?" Bess asked.

"No, I had already met him—but that's where we had our first date," I said. "Ned wanted to go out with me, but he had a test the next day, so I suggested we just meet in the Mahoney Library. He picked the spot: under the clock. He said it inspired him."

I actually met Ned Nickerson in junior high. He's studying English lit at the university. He's always loved to read; in fact, he has a habit of going to the library in his free time, closing his eyes, and picking out a book. Ned and his family used to live in Washington D.C., but his father gave up all of that to be the publisher of the *River Heights Bugle*. I'm glad he did, because otherwise, we wouldn't have met!

"I don't have a good story about the clock," Bess said, "but I have one about the jeweler who made it."

"If you're talking about the legend of the buried treasure, Bess, everyone's already heard it," George said, "and as far as I'm concerned, it's the sort of thing you only read about in old mystery books."

"Well, maybe—and then maybe not, George," I said. "There certainly are a lot of people in River Heights who believe it."

For as long as I can remember, one of the most talked-about legends of River Heights had to do with Ben Mullins and the library clock. When Mr. Mullins died almost penniless, his family was in shock. They all thought he was a wealthy man. After the funeral, several family members said that right before Mr. Mullins died, he started talking about spending all of his money on jewels and then burying them somewhere, but leaving a map showing the location so that his relatives would have to use their brains to find their inheritance. Mrs. Mullins told everyone that she just thought he was beginning to lose his mind and must be talking nonsense, but when it turned out that there was almost no money in their savings account, she began to believe that he had been telling the truth. So did a lot of other people in River Heights. For several months—so the story went—you'd see people all over town digging up vacant fields and the banks of the Muskoka River. According to the people who would talk about the treasure hunt, Mr. Mullins also left secret messages in some of the jewelry-store ads that he ran in the newspaper before he died. After a while most people stopped looking. Still, there was the occasional fortune hunter who was sure he knew where to look. If anyone ever found the buried treasure, though, they never talked about it.

"Thanks for agreeing to help me on the committee," I said. "I think we'll have a lot of fun."

Bess giggled. "Some of us will, at least," she said mysteriously.

"What do you mean?" I asked.

"Oh, Bess, cut it out," George said. She looked over at me. "My cousin here thinks I only agreed to be on the committee because of Ellis Lamsley."

I raised an eyebrow in surprise. "Who's Ellis Lamsley?" I asked.

George blushed, which is very unusual for her. "He's the new librarian," she said. "He's also a marathon runner who's placed in several meets in

5

the state, and I thought he might be willing to give me some pointers—after my committee work, of course."

"I didn't even know there was a new librarian," I said. "Lamsley. That's an unusual name."

"It's not that unusual, Nancy. I checked it out on the Internet—and I checked out Ellis," George said, her blush deepening. "Everything I had heard about him is true." She turned to Bess. "And you know, he fixes up old cars in his spare time. Maybe after he and I have run a few miles, you two could take apart his car and put it back together. Fun, fun!"

"Ha, ha, ha," Bess said.

Bess had actually gone on dates like that before. She never bragged about her talent for anything mechanical, but she had it—and she loved tinkering more than anyone I knew.

Just as we came up to the parking lot of one of the town's newest supermarkets, I remembered something I had to do. "I told Hannah that I'd pick up a couple of jars of pimentos for her," I told my friends, "and if I don't do it now, I'm sure I'll forget it."

I signaled to get into the right-hand lane, gave a friendly wave to the man who blasted his horn at me as I steered to the right and turned into the lot, then drove down the aisles until I found a parking space as close to the building as possible.

"I refuse to comment on what just happened," George said.

"Good," I said. "I'll be right back."

I jumped out of my car and hurried up to the front door. I was almost run over by one of those shopping carts in the form of a kiddie car. Just as I found the aisle where I thought the pimentos would be, I saw my friend Lucia Gonsalvo heading in my direction.

Any other time I would have been delighted to see her. Lucia is our own River Heights fortune-teller. She has a small shop downtown on River Street, and I usually love listening to her stories. But there was no time for stories now.

"Oh, Nancy! Nancy! It is fate that has brought us together next to the pickles!" Lucia called. She has an accent, but I've never been able to place it—and Lucia has never talked about where she lived before she moved to River Heights. "I have been thinking about you all morning, and they have not been good thoughts."

"Really, Lucia?" I said, preparing myself for one of her dramatic stories. "Why not?"

"Can't you see it? There is a dark cloud that surrounds your head!" Lucia said. "You must be very careful today. Something bad is just waiting to happen to you."

7

I looked up. Right above me one of the banks of lights was out. "There's your dark cloud, Lucia," I said.

"Oh, Nancy, Nancy, I guess I'm just being silly," Lucia said. She regarded me for a moment with her piercing dark eyes. "Still, I think you should be on your guard today."

"All right, Lucia," I said, "I promise that I'll pay very close attention to what's happening around me."

"Good," Lucia said. "You know I rarely feel this strongly—I just have a feeling you should be careful. Now, you'll find the pimentos at the end of this aisle."

How did she know? Well, I guess a lot of people knew my dad loved pimentos. . . . "Thanks," I said, casting her a questioning glance. "I'll see you later!"

I hurried past Lucia, found the pimentos, and took two jars from the top of a stack.

I paid for the pimentos and hurried back to my car. George had the door open and was starting to get out.

"What's wrong?" I asked.

"What's wrong?" George said. "You were taking forever!"

I explained about Lucia but didn't mention what she had told me.

"Did you see Deirdre in the store?" Bess asked.

"No, I didn't," I said. "Why?"

"Well, she arrived right after you left, parked in a handicap space, ran inside, then came back out with a small sack," Bess said.

"And while she was in the store, a car with a handicap tag drove by and couldn't find a place to park," George added.

"That's Deirdre for you," I said. I quickly hopped into the driver's seat. As I pulled out of the supermarket parking lot, I looked at my watch. "I told Mrs. Corning we'd be there at nine o'clock, when the library opens—and we'll make it with a couple of minutes to spare. Excellent."

"Who else is on the committee, Nancy?" Bess said.

"Just Ned—but I haven't told him yet," I said. "I think the four of us can handle everything that needs to be done, don't you?"

"Definitely," George said. "Anyway, I'd prefer to be on the committee with just you guys."

"Hey, Bess," I said, changing the topic, "I have a favor to ask. . . ."

"What is it?" Bess said.

"Well, Ned's parents are having a party tonight for a family friend from Washington D. C., and he's invited me," I explained. "It's dressy, so I was going to have you look over some of my outfits to tell me what you think goes best together."

Bess brightened. There's nothing she loves to do

more than help me coordinate my clothes. I personally like the simple, casual look—because, unlike Bess, haute couture has never been an interest of mine. For that night, though, I needed help.

"I'll help. And when I'm finished with you, everyone will think you just stepped from the pages of a fashion magazine!" Bess said.

I couldn't help but giggle.

"Who's the family friend?" George asked.

"Ned actually didn't tell me a name," I said, "but he's one of the president's advisers."

"What president?" Bess asked.

I looked at her. "*The* president," I said. "The one who lives in the White House."

"Oh, *that* president," Bess said.

I nodded. "Exactly," I said, pulling up to the library. "Well, we're here, so—wait, why are all those police cars in the library parking lot?"

George and Bess leaned forward and looked.

"Well, I'm sure it's not because Chief McGinnis is checking out a book to read!" George said.

I rolled my eyes at her. My friends are never very charitable about Chief McGinnis. Of course, he really is, well . . . kind of lazy, I guess you'd say. And he gets very irritated when I solve a mystery that's totally eluded him. Still, we try to be civil to each other. After all, he is the chief of police of River Heights!

I parked the car, and the three of us jumped out and headed toward the front of the library. Just as we reached the steps, Chief McGinnis opened the door and came out of the building.

When he saw us, he stopped and held up a hand. "I see you were listening to your police scanner again," he said.

I took a deep breath. Chief McGinnis always likes to tease that I have a police scanner and that I listen to it all the time, hoping to find a mystery to solve. Everyone knows I don't.

"No, we have a committee meeting here at the library this morning," I said, "but what's going on?"

"My officers and I have everything under control, Nancy," he said, "so you can just go on to your committee meeting."

I gave him one of my biggest smiles, trying to pretend I didn't know something was up. "Okay," I said.

"We'll all sleep better tonight, now that you're on the case!" George said, winking at me.

The three of us headed toward the front door, but Chief McGinnis stopped us with, "Okay, okay, I'll tell you—but you don't need to worry about trying to solve the case, because that's *my* job."

I stopped. "Well, of course!" I said. Excellent. Funny how all we had to do to get the chief to spill the beans sometimes was to act uninterested.

"Somebody stole the library clock last night," Chief McGinnis said. "Now there's just a big hole in the wall where it used to be."

What Else Can Go Wrong?

I couldn't believe it! Despite what I'd said just a moment ago, I had to find out what was going on. "See you later, Chief McGinnis," I said.

I opened the front door of the library and the three of us hurried inside. I didn't give Chief McGinnis a chance to tell me again how he had everything under control.

"Oh, this is awful!" Bess said. "Who would want to steal the library clock? I mean, who would have the heart?"

Ahead of us we saw Mrs. Corning at the circulation desk. She was literally pulling out her hair. Her normally perfect bun looked like a seeding dandelion, hairs drifting everywhere. She was also gesturing wildly at one of Chief McGinnis's officers.

"Mrs. Corning!" I shouted to her, momentarily forgetting that we were in a library and that I wasn't supposed to make a lot of noise.

Mrs. Corning looked in our direction. "Oh, Nancy, Nancy, Nancy!" she cried. "I'm so glad you're finally here!" She turned back to the officer. "Now, perhaps we'll be able to solve this crime!" she added in a hostile voice.

Uh-oh, I thought. I could see that her relationship with the police authority in River Heights was deteriorating rapidly. I picked up my pace and finally reached the counter.

"We just saw Chief McGinnis outside, and I'm thoroughly convinced that the investigation into the disappearance of the library clock is well under way," I said, nodding at the officer and giving him a smile. "Of course, I did offer my services, if he needed them—so he may be in touch with me."

Now, the officer looked puzzled, because I'm sure that he'd heard Chief McGinnis tell his officers a million times that he was tired of my meddling in River Heights police cases. But I'd fibbed more for Mrs. Corning's benefit than for the officer's. It seemed to calm her down.

"Well, all right," Mrs. Corning said. She faced the officer once again. "We can handle this now. There are probably a lot of other crimes in River Heights that need your attention."

"Yes, ma'am," the officer said. He actually seemed relieved to have been dismissed.

"Let's go to my office, girls," Mrs. Corning said. "How about a cup of hot tea to calm our nerves?"

"That sounds like a wonderful idea," Bess said.

My nerves actually felt fine, but I liked tea. And this gave me a chance to find out the story.

Mrs. Corning led us to the back of the circulation area. The front wall of her office is all a special kind of glass—she can see out, but no one can see in. Inside it's very nicely appointed, like you'd expect a room in her house to be. I know she spends a lot of time here, and I sometimes feel that's all my fault. Mrs. Corning and her husband are separated. He lives in California. Mrs. Corning's daughter, Helen, had always talked about becoming a movie star, so at my suggestion, she moved to California to live with her father in order to pursue her dream. Even though Mrs. Corning knew she'd be alone in River Heights, she put Helen's happiness first, but I knew she missed her daughter a lot.

Bess, George, and I sat down at a small table in a corner of the office, and Mrs. Corning served us English tea with scones and strawberry jam. It was all quite elegant.

"Do you feel like talking about what happened, Mrs. Corning?" I asked.

"Not really, Nancy—but I know we have to find the clock, or the seventy-fifth anniversary library celebration can't take place! And this is very important to Mrs. Mahoney," Mrs. Corning said, sniffing.

"Does Mrs. Mahoney know about the theft yet?" Bess asked.

Mrs. Corning nodded. "Someone at the library must have called her," she said. "When I talked to her maid, she said that Mrs. Mahoney was in her study looking glum. The celebration was also why Helen was planning to come home, because she has such fond memories of the library—and the clock. I was so looking forward to her visit!"

"Oh, that's wonderful," I said. "It'll be just like old times."

What a great idea for the theme of the celebration!

"Yes, but the clock was to be the focus of the celebration, Nancy—and if the star of the show isn't available, then why would Helen bother to come back to River Heights?" Mrs. Corning said.

That was a strange remark, I thought. Of course Helen missed her mother. But I was sure that Mrs. Corning didn't mean it the way it sounded.

"Well, we're not even going to think about that,

are we," Bess said. "Nancy'll find the clock, so the celebration can go on as planned."

Mrs. Corning reached across the table and grasped my hand. "Oh, Nancy, I knew I could count on you," she said with tears in her eyes.

"I'll do what I can," I said. I honestly did try to be diplomatic, as far as Chief McGinnis was concerned. "I have a pretty good relationship with the police department, so I think that with all of us working together, we'll find the library clock."

"Oh, come on! Chief McGinnis couldn't find his way out of a paper sack," Mrs. Corning said. "I just wish you were the only—"

Just then the door opened, causing us all to turn around.

"Oh, come on in, Ellis," Mrs. Corning said. She motioned to a chair across the room. "Bring that over here and join us for tea."

So *this* was Ellis Lamsley.

Ellis smiled and totally lit up the room. As he easily picked up the chair and started across the room, I couldn't help but watch. I've seen male models in fashion shows and on television that weren't this handsome. But I also noticed that right before Ellis reached us, he looked at himself in a mirror on the wall, double-checking his hair.

Yuck.

"Nancy, Bess, George—this is Ellis Lamsley, our new librarian," Mrs. Corning said. "Ellis, Nancy Drew and her two best friends, Bess Marvin and George Fayne."

"Well, it's a pleasure," Ellis said. He gave Bess one of those smiles that said, "I know you think I'm gorgeous and probably unavailable, but if you play your cards right, I might ask you out on a date."

Double yuck.

Bess gave him a coquettish smile, which I'm sure is exactly what Ellis expected. But I knew she saw *exactly* what I did, and was just being cordial.

"Nancy has agreed to help the police locate the library clock," Mrs. Corning said. "You're new in town, so you probably don't know anything about her detective skills."

"On the contrary," Ellis said smugly. "I've been spending time reading the microfilmed back issues of the *River Heights Bugle,* to familiarize myself with my new home. I've seen Nancy's name mentioned many times in the newspaper."

"Well," I said, "I think I get way too much credit in some of those news stories," I said, "but I do plead guilty to spending a lot of time trying to solve most of the mysteries of River Heights."

Ellis turned back to Mrs. Corning. "Well, I think

this case is in very good hands," he said. Then, lowering his voice to a whisper, he added, "I'm afraid I don't have too much faith in Chief McGinnis's ability to recover the clock."

"Ellis, I'm really impressed with all of the marathons you've won," George said, thankfully changing the topic. "I was thinking that maybe we could train together, so you could give me some pointers."

"Sure, why not," Ellis said. He looked at Bess. "Do *you* run?"

"It depends on who's chasing me, Ellis," Bess said. She winked at him.

Ellis wasn't prepared for that and almost lost his composure, but he grinned and recovered nicely. "I guess we'll just have to see what happens," he said. "We can make some plans after the committee meeting, if that's okay."

I gave Ellis a puzzled look.

"Oh, I'm sorry, Nancy," Mrs. Corning said. "I asked Ellis to serve on the committee with you. I hope that's all right."

"Oh, sure," I said, trying to sound positive, even though I didn't really feel that way. "The more the merrier."

"I think that would be great," George said.

"Do you run too, Nancy?" Ellis asked.

"Nancy already has a boyfriend, Ellis," Bess interjected.

At this, I was sure that I saw a quick flash of anger in Ellis's eyes. He wasn't used to a girl getting the best of him. He was used to girls melting at the sight of him. But I had to hand it to him; he got over it quickly. "Well, it didn't hurt to ask." He winked at all three of us.

"Thanks for the invitation anyway, Ellis," I said, looking around. I felt antsy, ready to start investigating—or planning. "Well, I think we all know one another well enough now that we can get down to business, so—"

Once more the door opened, and Willy Franklin, the janitor, stuck his head inside. "I found the note you left for me in my supply closet, Mrs. Corning," he said. "What did you want to see me about?"

"Come join us, Willy," Mrs. Corning said. "We're about to have a committee meeting about the library celebration."

"I don't know what's so special about this place that you have to celebrate it," Willy said sarcastically.

"Lots of things," I said. "The beautiful clock, for one."

Willy snorted on hearing that. "I guess you haven't seen that big hole in the wall," he said to me. He chuckled. "Is that what you're going to celebrate, Miss Drew?"

Like Bess, I can normally find *some* good in almost everyone—but I've always had to look really hard in Willy Franklin's case. He is one of the more unpleasant people I've ever met. He seems to resent everyone he comes in contact with—and it's been distracting in some of my investigations. It's hard not to suspect him of just about any crime.

"Nancy here plans to find the library clock before the celebration," Ellis told him. "In case you didn't know, she's quite the detective."

Shoot. Why did he have to say that? I knew what was coming next.

"I know all about Nancy Drew," Willy said. He walked over and sat down next to Mrs. Corning. He gave me a really hard stare. "But whoever stole that clock may be smarter than she is."

Like you, for instance, Mr. Franklin? I wanted to ask the question, but I didn't. *Could* Mr. Franklin be behind the theft of the library clock?

Willy Franklin leaned back in his chair, clasped his hands behind his head, and said, "If you ask me, I think you should just let me plaster up that hole in the wall and forget about the clock."

Mrs. Corning let out a gasp. "Well, that's certainly

not going to happen, so you can just get that silly idea out of your head," she said. She turned to me. "Nancy, will you please tell Willy what you'll be wanting him to do for the celebration? I'm sure he needs to leave so he can attend to other projects."

"Yeah, I need to get some sleep, so I can come back here tonight and clean this place up," Willy said.

I'd heard that Mr. Franklin had gotten in trouble over the last few years—arguments with neighbors that had occasionally turned into fistfights, things like that—but I honestly had no idea how completely rude Mr. Franklin could be. Actually, it wasn't just his rudeness—it was his insolence. Why was he tolerated at the library? It was amazing to me that something I had really been looking forward to, the library cele-bration, had now almost become drudgery, thanks to Ellis and Mr. Franklin.

I took a deep breath and let it out. Well, I was in charge of this—so it would be up to me to make sure it was successful. And I'd do just that. Somehow, I'd find the library clock, and somehow, I'd manage to work with these two men.

I gave Mr. Franklin one of my biggest smiles. Kill them with kindness, I always say. "Thank you for coming, Mr. Franklin. We all really appreciate it," I said. "We won't keep you. We'll be needing your help with the display cases, easels—things like that. I'm sure I'll want to move the ones that are already on the floor to different places, to highlight our displays. Mrs. Corning said there were other cases stored in the basement, so I'll take a look at them, then tag the ones I'd like you to clean and move up to the main library." I stopped and gave him another big smile. "So I guess that's really all for today. We really appreciate your coming."

Mr. Franklin shook his head and snorted, but he didn't comment. He just stood up and left the room.

"He is such an insolent man! If I thought I could get away with firing him, I would," Mrs. Corning said. "But he's got some connection to Mrs. Mahoney, through her husband, I think—so I never got rid of him. I wouldn't want to alienate Mrs. Mahoney."

"Oh, I think he probably has a good heart," Ellis said. I could tell the remark took everyone by surprise. "He's probably just unhappy about his status in life."

"He's certainly unhappy about *something*," George said.

"Does he have to be involved with this committee?" Bess asked.

"Well, I guess we could always move the display cases ourselves," I said.

"No, thanks," Bess said. "I'll just tune Mr. Franklin out."

"How long is Mr. Franklin here at the library by himself?" I said.

"About two hours. From ten P.M., when the library closes, until midnight, when his shift is over," Mrs. Corning said. "Why?"

"I was just curious," I said.

Ellis looked at me. "I just don't think Willy could have had anything to do with the disappearance of the library clock, if that's what you're thinking, Nancy," he said. "I know he's really unpleasant, but frankly, I doubt if he's bright enough to figure out how to pull off a crime like this. Just like he said, it was someone clever."

Before I could respond to Ellis's remark, a voice at the door said, "Sorry I'm late! Did I miss anything important?"

I felt my stomach drop. The voice belonged to Deirdre Shannon.

"Oh, hi, DeeDee," I said. She hates that nickname. "What are you late for, and why would you think you missed anything?"

"I'm on your committee, Nancy," Deirdre said, breezing into the room and sitting down in the seat vacated by Mr. Franklin.

I was finding it almost impossible to say anything. I looked at Mrs. Corning. All I was able to say was, "I didn't know."

"Oh, I'm sorry, dear. The library clock theft has me so rattled, I can't seem to remember anything," Mrs. Corning said. "Deirdre called this morning and offered her services. Since I know how much work this is going to be, I was sure you wouldn't mind."

What a disaster. The library clock was gone, Mr. Franklin was going to be impossible to work with, and Deirdre would be around to make our lives miserable. What else could go wrong?

3

Ralph Mullins's Threat

Between gritted teeth, I managed, "We're delighted to have you, Deirdre, but try to be on time for all the future meetings."

Deirdre gave me a smirk. "Well, actually, I was on time, Nancy," she said. "In fact, I was here before you and your friends were."

"Really?" I said. "Well, then, where were you?"

"It's my fault, Nancy," Mrs. Corning said. "When Deirdre got here, things were in such chaos, because we had just discovered that the clock was missing— so I asked her if she would help the children's librarian shelve books." She gave Deirdre a big librarian smile. "Without any hesitation whatsoever, she agreed to do it."

Oh, brother. Deirdre Shannon, *library assistant?*

"Well, that was nice of you, Deirdre," Bess said. She turned to George. "Isn't that really nice of Deirdre?"

"Why, yes, it really is," George said. She looked at Deirdre. "We were just talking about you this morning, when we saw you pulling into that parking space at the supermarket. We were just saying what a nice, thoughtful, sensitive person Deirdre Shannon was. You know the type of person we're talking about. The one who helps little old ladies and gentlemen across the street. The one who would never park in a handicap parking space. The one who . . . well, you get the picture."

Deirdre turned bright red.

"Well," I said, "I guess we'd better start our meeting. What I think we should do first is—"

"Ned is really disappointed that you didn't want him on the committee, Nancy," Deirdre said, interrupting. "Actually, I am too, because I think he always has really good ideas."

"What do you mean, Deirdre?" I said. "He *is* on the committee." I didn't add that I hadn't told him yet.

Deirdre eyed me suspiciously.

"Anyway, when were you talking to Ned?" I asked.

Deirdre gave everyone her I'm-in-control-here smile and said, "This morning, at the student union, when I had an early breakfast with a friend of mine.

I told Ned I was really sorry that you didn't want him on the committee."

"Why did you tell him that, Deirdre?" I asked.

"Because it's true!" Deirdre said. "Ned hadn't heard anything about this committee, Nancy!" she added triumphantly. "You were just saying that."

"It isn't true, Deirdre," I said, turning to everyone else. "Ned Nickerson is on this committee too, but he had an English lit test this morning, so he wasn't able to attend this first meeting. I'll see him tonight, so I'll fill him in on everything we talked about."

Of course, I wasn't really lying. Every time Ned and I were together recently, he was studying for another exam. How could I have a chance to tell him?

Bess and George smirked.

"Perhaps he just *forgot,* Nancy," Deirdre said sarcastically. She was still eyeing me suspiciously. "If you'd like me to, I can fill Ned in before then."

The girl never gives up!

"I'll probably see him this afternoon at the university library," Deirdre continued. She looked at everyone else. "My friend works in circulation," she added. "I'm at the library a lot. So is Ned."

"Why, thank you, Deirdre! That's a wonderful idea!" I said. "I'll take you up on that." I'd just explain it all to Ned later. He'd understand. He might even think he really had just forgotten. He's used to how I operate.

I could tell that Deirdre was a little surprised at how easily I accepted her offer, but she didn't question it.

Now Bess and George were looking at me as though I had lost my mind. But see, there is no way to win with Deirdre. The only way she'll ever stop flirting with Ned will be if somebody locks her in her room—without a telephone—for the rest of her life. Of course, Ned is immune to what she thinks are her charms. I'd go ahead and let Deirdre give Ned her version of the meeting, and then I'd give him the real version later.

Mrs. Corning's office was beginning to feel claustrophobic. "The first thing I want us to do," I said, slipping back into my role as chair of the committee, "is to take a tour of the library to see just where we should put all the displays."

"That's an excellent idea, Nancy," Ellis said. He stood up and turned to Mrs. Corning. "I'll be happy to take everyone around, if you have some other things you need to attend to."

"Oh, Ellis, thank you, I do," Mrs. Corning said. "With all the chaos this morning, I forgot that I have to make out the budget to give to Mrs. Mahoney. She likes to look at it before she gives it to her lawyer."

Just as Ellis opened the door, I heard an unfamiliar buzzing noise. The source stopped us in our tracks. The library looked more like the mall on a Saturday afternoon than it did a library.

"Good grief!" Mrs. Corning said. "What is going on?"

"I think I know. The news about the library clock has gotten out," I said. "It looks as though everyone in River Heights has come here to see the scene of the crime."

"Well, we can't have this," Mrs. Corning said. "We simply can't."

"It's a library, Mrs. Corning, open to the public," Ellis reminded her. "I don't think you can ask them to leave."

Ellis was right. The noise was a little louder than you'd expect in a library reading room, but it certainly wasn't as loud as it could have been, given the size of the crowd.

"I have an idea," I said. "Let's use this crowd to our advantage."

"How?" Deirdre demanded. "They just look like a bunch of stupid people to me."

"Oh, really, Deirdre?" George said. She turned to Bess. "Isn't that the mayor of River Heights pointing to the hole in the wall?"

"Why, I do believe it is, George," Bess said. "I also

see Mr. Nickerson, Harold Safer, and Evaline Waters." She looked at Deirdre. "I don't think they'd appreciate being referred to as stupid people."

Deirdre looked as though she might explode, she was getting so angry.

"Oh, there's your father, too, Deirdre," I added.

"I think we should stick to a tour of the library," Deirdre said. "We're already behind schedule."

"What was your idea, Nancy?" Mrs. Corning said.

"Well, these people obviously are very upset that the library clock has been stolen, or they wouldn't have left their businesses to come here," I said. "That means they probably have their own stories about the library clock."

"Right," Bess said. "Just like the stories we were telling one another on the way over here."

I nodded. "You know, I think their stories of what the clock means to them would make a great display," I continued. "While they're here, let's get each one of them to sit down at the tables and write down whatever they can remember."

"How could a silly clock mean anything to anybody?" Deirdre asked. "Won't stories about how you looked up to see what time it was be kind of boring?"

"Well, I guess we'll find out, won't we?" I said. "Mrs. Corning, do you have some pads and pencils we could use?"

"Of course," Mrs. Corning said. "I keep a supply for our children's activities."

"Nancy, you and Ellis go ahead and tell everyone what you want them to do," Bess said. "The rest of us will get the pads and pencils."

"Thanks, Bess," I said.

Ellis and I headed toward the crowd of people all pointing at the huge hole in the wall of the library. "Let's talk to Mr. Nickerson first," I said. "Since he's used to doing newspaper stories, I doubt if he'll say no when we ask him to write down his favorite memories of the library clock."

"Good thinking, Nancy," Ellis said. "When the rest of the people see what he's doing, they may be more willing to do the same thing."

I hoped so. "Mr. Nickerson!" I called.

Mr. Nickerson looked up. "Oh, hi, Nancy," he said. He nodded toward the hole in the library wall. "Isn't this just awful? Such a tragedy."

"It is," I said, "but I'm sure it'll return soon."

"Let's hope so," Mr. Nickerson said.

"With Nancy Drew on the case, it's a done deal," Ellis said.

"Oh, I'm sorry!" I said, remembering my manners. "Mr. Nickerson, this is Ellis Lamsley, the new librarian."

"It's a pleasure to meet you, Ellis," Mr. Nickerson said.

"The pleasure is all mine," Ellis said. "I'm a big fan of your newspaper."

"Thanks," Mr. Nickerson said.

"When I read your editorials about the president and Congress, I don't feel as though I'm in a small town," Ellis said. "They're more like something you'd find in one of the Washington D.C. newspapers."

Mr. Nickerson smiled. "Oh, really? Well, I'm glad I haven't lost my touch."

Ellis looked puzzled.

"The Nickersons used to live in Washington," I said. "Mr. Nickerson was a very famous investigative reporter."

Ellis looked impressed.

"Mr. Nickerson, as you know, the library's seventy-fifth anniversary is coming up," I said, "and I'm the chair of one of the celebration committees."

Mr. Nickerson nodded his head toward the hole in the wall. "Well, there's going to be something important missing from the celebration, isn't there?" he said.

I nodded. "That's why I thought I'd get as many people as possible to write down what the library clock means to them, and I wanted you to be the first," I said. "Would you be willing to do that?"

"Of course," Mr. Nickerson said. "I'm embarrassed to admit, though, that I'm here without my reporter's notebook. Do you have anything—"

"Here we are," Bess said, walking up to us. Deirdre and George were right behind her, their hands full of pencils and spiral notebooks.

I took a set, and handed it to Mr. Nickerson.

"Ned was fascinated with the library clock when he was a boy," Mr. Nickerson said. "It was similar to the one in Washington that helped him first learn how to tell time."

"I didn't know that," I said, smiling.

"Oh, yes," Deirdre said. "It's such a cute story."

We all turned and looked at her.

"What?" Deirdre said.

While Mr. Nickerson wrote down his clock story, the rest of us circulated through the crowd, asking other people to tell theirs. I kept myself as far away from Deirdre as possible.

As we had expected, some people declined our request—but many others weren't so shy.

Suddenly I spotted Evaline Waters at the edge of the crowd. She was wiping her eyes with a dainty handkerchief. I hurried over to her. Ms. Waters is the first librarian I ever knew, and she's still my favorite. I miss having her at the River Heights Public Library. She's now retired, and lives in a little house just a few blocks from the Mahoney Library. She must have heard the noise, and come by to see what the hubbub was about.

"Ms. Waters!" I called, walking up to her.

Ms. Waters looked up. "Oh, Nancy, this is such a tragedy! I just don't know what to—"

"Pardon me—I have an announcement to make!"

I turned around. An elderly man was standing at the edge of the crowd. "Who is that?" I asked.

"Oh, my goodness," Ms. Waters said. "That's Ralph Mullins!" She looked back at me. "He's the son of Ben Mullins, the jeweler who made the clock and donated it to the Mahoney Library."

Mrs. Corning and the rest of the librarians had stepped out of their offices.

Ralph Mullins turned toward them. "It's *your* fault that this clock is missing, Frances!" he shouted. "Have you forgotten about the agreement that the library signed with my father?"

"Oh, no," Ms. Waters whispered, turning pale.

What was going on here?

"Well, I'll remind you," Mr. Mullins shouted. "It says that if you don't take good care of the clock, then it reverts to my family!" He smiled. "We've hired a private detective. When he finds the clock, it'll be ours!"

4

Ned Has a Plan

You can imagine how stunned everybody was. We all just stood there and watched Ralph Mullins stalk out of the library.

When I looked over at Mrs. Corning I saw she had an expression of terror on her face. I hurried over to her.

"Are you all right?" I asked.

Mrs. Corning blinked a couple of times. "Am I all right? *Am I all right?* Nancy! If the library loses that clock, then I'll probably lose my job. How would Mrs. Mahoney understand? So, no, I'm not all right." With that, she rushed away, sobbing hysterically.

Just then Ellis walked up. "I think she's pretty close to a nervous breakdown, don't you?"

I let out a deep sigh. It was really unlike Mrs.

Corning to blow up like this. Now, I knew I should probably go see if she was all right—but at the same time, I kind of wanted to stick around. This was getting intense.

A couple of the other librarians looked as though they were headed toward Mrs. Corning's office, so I felt that I was off the hook. But I did suddenly wonder why Ellis hadn't suggested that somebody look in on her.

"Is this enough, Nancy?"

When I turned around, Ms. Waters was holding out several sheets of paper with her fine handwriting. "I wrote down everything I could think of," she said.

"Oh, thank you so much, Ms. Waters," I said. "That will really help the display a lot." I hesitated a minute. "Is it really true, what Mr. Mullins said?" I asked. "Does the clock revert to his family if the library doesn't take care of it?"

Ms. Waters nodded. "I'm afraid it is," she said, shrugging. "When Ben Mullins gave the clock to the library, and a contract was drafted, he had the clause included—and the library didn't notice. If anyone had suggested at the time that the clock would ever be stolen, they would have been laughed at." She shook her head sadly. "Well, I need to be going. This has already been quite a morning. I'm not used to this much excitement anymore."

"Thank you again," I said, but then I thought of something. "Wait a minute! As chair of the decoration committee, I'm connected to the library—so if I find the clock, then I can say that the library really is 'taking care of it,' can't I?"

"That's true, Nancy," Ms. Waters said. "It's a stretch, but I'm sure that your father could make the case in court that you're right." She took my hand and patted it. "I wouldn't doubt that Nancy Drew would be able to solve the mystery of the library clock," she said.

With that, she headed out of the library.

"Good thinking, Nancy," Ellis said. "Shall we help Bess and George collect the rest of the essays?"

"Yes, let's do that," I said.

It turned out that Bess and George had already collected everything that everyone had written. Several people had decided they didn't want to write down their recollections after all, so there weren't as many as I had thought there would be. But what we had would still make an interesting display.

"Where's Deirdre?" I asked.

"Oh, she said she needed to go to the university library," Bess said nonchalantly. "She thought that Ned should hear right away about everything that's happened."

"Oh, of course," I said. I rolled my eyes. "What was I thinking?"

"Right," Bess said. "What were you thinking?"

"If you don't need us for anything else, Nancy, we should run too," George said. "I have some work I need to do on the computer for Mom."

"We're through here for today," I said. "I'll call you after Ned brings me home tonight."

"Oh, I forgot about that," Bess said. "I told you I'd help you pick out an outfit to wear."

"That's okay, Bess," I said. "I'll try this once to manage!"

"I'm sure you'll *manage,* Nancy. You always *manage,*" Bess said. She grinned. "The question is, manage to do *what*?"

"Okay, okay, enough!" I said, smiling. "I promise I won't try to make any obscene fashion statements."

After Bess and George were gone, I turned to Ellis for some more information about the clock. "Tell me, why is the Mullins family so interested in getting back the library clock?" I asked. "It's beautiful, but it's really too big for a house. What would they do with it?"

"Sell it," Ellis said.

"Sell it?" I said. "That's awful!"

Ellis shrugged. "Well, seems to me they're awful people, Nancy," he said. "That clock would probably bring in a lot of money if it was put on the market."

"You're probably right about that," I said. "Well, that definitely gives me even more incentive to find it. That clock was made for the Mahoney Library. It wasn't made for anybody else."

"Still, Ben Mullins insisted that the clause appear in the agreement," Ellis said.

I looked at him. "You certainly know a lot about this, just to have recently arrived in River Heights," I said.

"I'm a *librarian*, Nancy. That means I work in a library, and there are all kinds of interesting things in a library besides books," Ellis said. "Ben Mullins left all his papers, diaries, drawings, sketches, sales receipts— you name it—to the Mahoney Library, and I've been going through everything."

"Really?" I said.

Ellis nodded. "When I found out that the clock was to be the focal point of the anniversary celebration, I thought I might find something you could use," he said.

"Well, that's nice of you," I said. I thumbed through the papers in my hand. "There may not be enough of these personal recollections for more than one display, so it's nice to know that other things are available." I thought for a minute. "Maybe tomorrow we can look through some of the sketches," I added. "Let me think about it."

"Okay," Ellis said. He looked at his watch. "Well, I'd better get back to work myself."

"See you later," I said. I put the recollections on

the desk Mrs. Corning had told me to use and I left.

When I got home, I took the pimentos out of the car, gave them to Hannah, then filled her in on what had happened.

"Oh, my goodness, that's awful, Nancy," Hannah said. "That is such a pretty clock!"

It suddenly occurred to me that maybe Hannah had a clock story she could write down for me, but before I could ask her, she said, "I think I'm going to need another jar of pimentos. Do you think you could pick up one for me before you go see Ned?"

"Before I go see Ned?" I said. "What do you mean?"

"Oh, he called right before you came in and asked if you could meet him in the Asian foods area of the university union food court this afternoon," Hannah said. "When you told me about the library clock, it just slipped my mind for a minute. He needed to talk to you about something."

"Deirdre," I muttered.

"Oh, my goodness," Hannah said. "Has that girl finally managed to create problems for you two?"

"Oh, you know that would never happen, Hannah," I said. "It's just that, well . . . It's a long, boring story, and I need to shower before I go. If it turns out to be anything more than what I think it is, I'll fill you in tonight, okay?"

"Sounds good," Hannah said.

41

There was just one visitor's parking space in front of the new university union, and I quickly pulled into it. I was already ten minutes late, so I ran up the steps and through the automatic doors, then headed toward the food court. I saw Ned right away, head buried in a book, totally oblivious to the noise around him.

"Hi!" I said, walking up to the table.

When Ned didn't respond, I grinned. What a bookworm. I punched him on the shoulder and said, "Sorry, I'm late." I pulled out a chair and sat down.

"Oh, Nancy, sorry," Ned said. He grinned, showing his dimples. It's easy to see why Deirdre and almost every other girl in River Heights flirts with Ned. He's *so* good-looking. "I was rereading this great poem. Listen." He paused for a moment, then began. "'Shall I compare thee to a summer's day? . . .'"

Now this was pure Ned Nickerson. A major catastrophe could be about to happen, but Ned will make sure it gets delayed if he's found a poem that appeals to him. I've never known anyone else who can read a poem and make me feel that it was written especially for me. This was a Shakespeare sonnet, number eighteen. By the time he finished with "this gives life to thee," my heart was pounding.

"Oh, Ned, that was beautiful," I said. "Thank you."

"You're welcome," Ned said. "Now, what's this about my being on your library committee?"

"I'm sorry about that, Ned. If you really don't have time, I'll understand," I said. "I'd been meaning to ask you, but you were always so busy, and now, with the library clock gone, I'm going to have my mind on more than just decorating for the celebration. But I know I should have asked you first."

"What, and spoil your reputation for surprises?" Ned said, winking. "You know you can count on me, Nancy."

"Yes, I do, Ned," I said. "Okay, let me fill you in on what we—"

"Actually," he interrupted, "Deirdre did a pretty good job of that already. The reason I wanted to meet you here is that I've been doing some sleuthing on my own, and I've uncovered some information that I think you'll be interested in."

Ned's not really into mysteries the same way I am, but he's always ready to help me out with whatever I'm investigating. Since his head is full of all kinds of details, more than once he's given me just the right piece of information to put all the pieces of the puzzle together.

"Great!" I said. "Let's hear it."

"Well, it's about Ralph Mullins," Ned said. "He's—"

"Oh, you should have been there, Ned," I cut in. "It was all so odd!"

Ned shook his head. "I can imagine," he said. "Anyway, I decided to do a little research on him, and I found out some really interesting things."

I leaned closer. "What did you find out?"

"First of all, Ralph Mullins is in debt over his head," Ned said. "If he doesn't come up with a lot of money fast, he could lose his home. Also, Ralph Mullins works here at the university. He's a locksmith."

"A locksmith?" I asked. "Is he in charge of making the keys for the university?"

Ned nodded. "Don't you find that interesting?"

"Sure do," I said.

"That means it probably wouldn't be much of a problem for him to make a key to fit one of the Mahoney Library doors," Ned added.

Just what I was thinking. "Do you think Ralph Mullins stole the clock himself, so he could 'find it' and then sell it for a lot of money?"

5

Guilt by Association

I looked at my watch. It was four o'clock. And now, I had a plan that, I hoped, would help us recover the library clock.

A few weeks ago, when Ned's car wouldn't start, he called me, frantic to get to the library to check some sources before a class discussion. Thanks to that trip, I knew that the maintenance workers start an hour before most of the other university employees—they work from 7 A.M. until 4 P.M. That meant that Ralph Mullins was just getting off work.

"Come on, Ned," I said. "It's time to do some work!"

"Nancy, I'm not through reviewing for this test tomorrow," Ned said.

"Bring along your notes when you pick me up for

the party tonight," I said. "I'll quiz you after we get bored and want to go."

Ned laughed. "You'd do that?" he said. He sounded genuinely surprised—and pleased.

"Of course!" I told him. "You should know that."

Ned stood up, gathered his papers, and said, "Okay, then. Where are we going?"

"Ralph Mullins's house," I replied.

"Okay, but let's take my car, Nancy," Ned said. "That way you can concentrate on sleuthing."

"What's the matter, Ned?" I said, giving him a big grin. "Don't you think I can drive and sleuth at the same time?"

"Uh . . . no comment," Ned said.

Ned's car was parked on the opposite side of the university union from mine. He used the remote to open it, and we got inside.

As we headed out of the parking lot, something hit me. "Oh, great," I said. "I don't even know where Ralph Mullins lives. What was I thinking?"

"Open the glove compartment. You'll find a miniature city telephone directory inside," Ned said. "I'm always doing errands for Dad, so it really comes in handy."

That's my boyfriend. Always prepared. I got out the directory, turned to the *M*s, and found Ralph Mullins's address. I read it out to Ned.

"That's not too far from here," he said. "I know the area. It has inexpensive but well-kept houses."

I was looking up ahead. "What kind of vehicle would you think Ralph Mullins drives?" I asked.

Ned shrugged. "There's no telling," he said. "If he and his family are hurting for money, then it's probably not a brand-new luxury car."

"What about an old pickup truck?" I said.

"That would fit. A lot of the maintenance people at the university drive those," Ned said. "Why?"

"Because there's one up ahead of us with a university parking sticker on the back window," I said, pointing. "It looks like the driver's headed where we're headed."

Ned looked. "That could be anybody, Nancy," he said. "There are probably other people who work for the university who live in that neighborhood too."

"Get closer so we can find out for sure, Ned," I said.

"You want me to tailgate?" Ned said.

"No. Just get close enough so I can see through the rear window," I said. "I want to know if that's Ralph Mullins."

Ned sped up, but he kept a safe distance between us and the old pickup.

Finally I was able to peek into the driver's seat. "It is!" I said.

"How can you tell from this distance, Nancy?"

Ned asked. "There's no way you can see his face."

"I don't have to see his face, Ned. I can still picture the back of his head as he stalked out of the library," I said. "We were all so stunned, we just stood there and watched. It's solidly imprinted in my memory."

Ned suddenly turned a corner and headed down a side street.

"Where are you going?" I asked.

"If Ralph Mullins thinks we're following him, he might get suspicious," Ned said, "so now that we know who it is, we'll come to his house from a different direction."

"Good thinking."

The part of town we were in now was really a hodgepodge of streets going at all kinds of weird angles, but we finally managed to find our way out and back onto a street that I knew would take us to Ralph Mullins's house.

Ned let his car crawl down the street, so we could do a little spying. When Ralph got out of his pickup, he seemed to be having an angry conversation on a cell phone. Suddenly a woman whom I assumed was his wife came out the front door and started shouting something at him. Ralph Mullins gestured for her to be quiet, but she kept yelling. As we slowly passed, I turned around so I could see what else was going to happen. Now the woman seemed even angrier, but then, so did Mr. Mullins. Without saying anything to the woman, he got back into his pickup and pealed out of the driveway. I'm glad he was headed away from us, because I don't think he was looking where he was going.

I turned back around. "That is one angry man, for sure," I said to Ned.

Ned nodded. "He could be under a lot of pressure from his family to bring in more money," he said. He was looking in his rearview mirror. "I'd say Ralph Mullins was capable of stealing anything he thought he could make some money off of, including a library clock," he said.

I nodded. "I think you're right about that, Ned," I said.

"Where to now, Nancy?"

I took out the telephone directory, turned to the Fs, and ran my finger down a column. "Nine twenty-two Cleveland Street," I said.

"That's on the opposite side of River Heights, Nancy," Ned said. "Who lives there?"

"Willy Franklin," I replied. "The janitor at the library."

I had suddenly thought of how the library clock could have disappeared. As we headed in the direction of Willy Franklin's house, I told Ned about how the janitor had acted this morning during the committee meeting. "All he wants to do is plaster over the hole in the wall and forget about the clock."

"It definitely sounds like he's trying to get people to think it's not worth finding," Ned said.

I grinned at him. Why would you want to find something, if you already knew where it was?

Ned grinned back. He knew that I might just have put together some pieces of the puzzle, but he didn't ask me to explain what they were. That's another thing I like about him: he just lets me think when I need to think.

"What do we do now?" Ned asked. "Park? Drive by slowly? Get out and stroll past? What?"

I looked at my watch. "Mr. Franklin's shift at the library starts at six P.M., so he could still be home," I said. "Slow down a little, so I can get a good look, but not so much that we look like we're casing his house, on the chance he's standing at the window."

I began reading the house numbers out loud. "It should be the next one," I said. When we reached it, I saw that Mr. Franklin had a carport instead of a garage, so it was easy to tell that he wasn't at home.

"Maybe he had some errands to do before he went to work," Ned suggested.

"Or," I said, finally giving Ned the pieces of the

puzzle I had put together, "maybe he knows Ralph Mullins, and maybe Mr. Mullins was talking to him on the telephone when we saw him getting out of his pickup!"

"That's kind of a stretch, isn't it, Nancy?" Ned said.

"Why? Stranger things have happened, Ned," I said. "Together they easily could have hatched a plan to steal the clock."

Ned thought about that for a minute. "Yeah, actually, that makes sense."

"Maybe the fact that Ralph Mullins is a locksmith has nothing to do with breaking into the library to steal the clock," I continued. "He could have reminded Mr. Franklin of the library's agreement to take care of the clock, and convinced him to help Mullins with the robbery. Mr. Franklin could simply have let him in after hours so the two of them could take it out of the wall."

"Right!" Ned agreed. "Ralph Mullins would then give Mr. Franklin part of the money that he made when he sold it."

I nodded. "I wonder where they would be meeting now."

"I guess we should have followed Mr. Mullins when he left," Ned said. "Sorry, Nancy."

"Don't be sorry, Ned. It's not your fault," I said. "I

hadn't fit the last piece of the puzzle when I told you to drive over to Mr. Franklin's house."

Ned looked at his watch. "Now what?" he asked.

"I don't think there's anything else we can do now. Why don't you just take me back to my car, so I can go home and get cleaned up for the party tonight," I suggested. "I also want to talk to Dad about the case. He may have some more ideas."

"Home it is," Ned said.

I pulled into our driveway right behind Dad, so we headed into the house together. I started immediately to fill him in on the case, and on the way to his study, we paused at the kitchen door. "We're home, Hannah!" Dad said. "Something smells good."

"It's almost ready," Hannah said. "I thought you were still going to Ned's, Nancy, so there's just enough here for your father. But if you're not, it won't be any trouble to—"

"No, no, you're fine, Hannah," I said, interrupting. "Ned and I still have plans for tonight."

As we continued on toward Dad's study, I thought about how really lucky I am to have Carson Drew as a father. We have a great relationship, one that a lot of my friends are really envious of. Of course, it's also nice that my father is one of the most prominent attorneys in River Heights. Besides the normal father-daughter things we talk about, we also discuss each other's cases in general terms—only when the information is pertinent, of course. I only run into problems when a case is risky; Dad doesn't want to hear all the details about the dangers I face.

As Dad set his briefcase down on his desk, I decided to jump right in, asking some of the questions I had for him. "Dad, do the names Ralph Mullins or Willy Franklin mean anything to you?"

"Isn't Mr. Franklin the janitor at the Mahoney Library?" Dad said.

I nodded. "Yes, he is," I replied.

"Well, that's the extent of my information about him, but Ralph Mullins is another story," Dad said.

I arched an eyebrow. "Oh, really?" I said. "Is it anything you can talk about?"

"There's no attorney-client relationship, if that's what you mean," Dad said. "In fact, it was one of *my* clients who Ralph Mullins tried to swindle out of a lot of money several years ago."

"This is sounding more and more promising," I said. I finished telling Dad about the events of the morning, and then about what Ned and I had seen that afternoon. "What happened to your case—the one that involved Ralph?" I asked.

"My client's doctor convinced his family that a trial would be harmful to his health, so they moved him to a nursing home in Oklahoma and dropped the charges," Dad said. "He was already sick when it began."

"That's too bad," I said.

"Yes, it is," Dad said. "I can tell you this much, Nancy," he continued. "During the preliminary hearings for my case, I heard all about Ralph Mullins and the schemes he's been involved in over the years. He seems like the kind of man who is always thinking up illegal ways to make money."

Ned's family friend was delayed in Washington at the last minute, so the party that night was canceled. Ned and I decided to go to Pizza Mia, one of the best brick-oven pizzerias in River Heights. I filled him in on what Dad had told me about Ralph Mullins, and then I quizzed him over and over on the questions he was sure would be on his test the next day. We were the last ones to leave the restaurant—but since Ned and I go there often, the owner doesn't mind if we hang around till closing.

I didn't realize how tired I actually was until I woke up the next morning with a start. Hannah was knocking on my door.

"I hate to disturb you, Nancy, but Bess, George, and a really nice-looking young man are waiting for you in the living room," she said. "Bess said you had a library committee meeting this morning."

"Oh, I do! I guess I forgot to set my alarm last night," I said. "Will you tell them I'll be out in just a couple of minutes?"

"Okay, dear," Hannah said.

I quickly showered, dressed, and made myself as presentable as I could in a short period of time. But really, I can't win when it comes to fashion. When I went into the living room, Bess had a comment. "Nancy," she said, "we really don't mind waiting until you get ready—"

I rolled my eyes. "I *am* ready, Bess!" I said.

Bess actually blushed. She'd been serious. "Oops!"

George and Ellis were dressed in track suits. "I see you two have been out running," I said.

"Well, we didn't actually make it to the track," George said. I detected some anger in her voice, so I knew that something had happened to irritate her.

"It's my fault," Ellis said with a wide smile. "I just got to talking to Bess about all kinds of different things, and the time just got away from us."

I was getting the picture. George had made a date with Ellis to run in the park. Ellis, who couldn't stand it if a girl didn't fall all over him, decided that it was more important to bring Bess into his camp than to honor his promise to run with George. What a jerk.

Just then I heard the telephone ring. Since I knew Ned was taking a test, and the only other people who call me were both standing in front of me, I doubted it was for me. I was wrong.

Hannah appeared at the door to the living room. "Nancy, it's Mrs. Corning," she said. "She sounds really upset about something."

I went into the kitchen and picked up the receiver. "Good morning, Mrs. Corning," I said, as cheerfully as I could.

"There's nothing good about it, Nancy," Mrs. Corning said. "Everyone's stories are gone—and now we have no theme for the celebration. And you're aware of our tight deadline. I'm afraid your carelessness is going to ruin the library celebration!"

6

This Is Not a Coincidence!

I was so stung by Mrs. Corning's accusation that I couldn't speak at first—and before I could find any words, my ear was assaulted by a loud dial tone. Mrs. Corning had hung up.

"What's wrong, Nancy?" Hannah asked. "From the look on your face, I know that wasn't good news."

"Hannah, this library celebration is turning into a nightmare," I managed to say. "I'm beginning to think that I'm one of those people who brings everyone bad luck."

"Nancy Drew! What are you talking about?" Hannah exclaimed. "I have several scrapbooks of newspaper clippings, where people you've helped over the years are praising you to the skies. We can look at them again if you need to . . ."

Hannah threatens to pull out the scrapbooks whenever I'm feeling frustrated. But that wasn't really what I needed at that moment. "That's okay. But, well, my luck may have just run out," I said. I still couldn't believe how angry Mrs. Corning had sounded. "I'll tell you more about it later."

When I got back to the living room, I saw that my friends had heard me talking to Hannah. They looked pretty worried. "I have to go to the library," I said. "It's kind of an emergency. Do you three want to ride with me?"

Ellis looked at his watch. "I would, Nancy, but I have the morning off, and I wanted to do some errands after George and I ran this morning." He turned to George and shrugged. "Sorry we didn't make it to the track," he said. "What about later today?"

"I can't," George said. She must have realized how frosty that sounded, so she added, "But I'll call you tomorrow and see if we can set up something else."

"Okay," Ellis said. He gave her one of his big smiles. Frankly, it seemed even phonier now than the first time I saw him do it. "You're welcome to join us," he said to Bess.

"I'll pass, Ellis," Bess said, then turned immediately to me. "Let's take care of this emergency."

Out of the corner of one eye, I saw Ellis frown—but he quickly covered it up.

"See everyone later," Ellis said.

"Okay," I said.

I waited until Ellis had let himself out before I filled my friends in. "That was Mrs. Corning," I said. "It seems that all the remembrances about the clock that everyone wrote down yesterday have disappeared."

"What?" Bess and George said in unison.

"How could that have happened?" George said.

"Mrs. Corning said it was because of my carelessness," I told them.

"Mrs. Corning said that?" Bess said.

I nodded. "I put those papers on the desk she assigned me in the Reference Section," I said. "She said that desk was safe—for library staff only. But someone must have taken them deliberately."

"Who would do that?" George asked.

"That's what we're going to find out," I said. "Come on!"

We went out to the garage, got into my car, and headed to the library.

When we arrived, we went straight to Mrs. Corning's office. She was just hanging up the telephone. She saw us and motioned us inside.

"Have a seat, girls," Mrs. Corning said. She stood up, came around from behind the desk, and sat down with us.

"Mrs. Corning, I am positive that I put those recollections that people wrote about the clock on top of the desk you assigned me," I began. "I remember doing it. I just don't understand how this happened."

"Perhaps you just *think* you did that, Nancy," Mrs. Corning countered. "Yesterday was quite a strain on all of us. Maybe you just absentmindedly put them in the wastebasket instead of on top of the desk—because that's where Mr. Franklin found them."

"*Mr. Franklin?*" I said. I looked at Bess and George.

"Yes," Mrs. Corning said. "I had to call him this morning about another matter, and that's when he mentioned the recollections."

"What did he say?" George asked.

"He said that last night, when he was cleaning up the library, he saw them in the wastebasket by Nancy's assigned desk," Mrs. Corning said. "He told me that he thought at the time that it was strange, since Nancy made such a big production out of getting people to write down what they remembered about the old library clock—but he said he just decided that you had changed your mind."

"No, I hadn't changed my mind, and I would not have just thrown those papers away," I said angrily. "Somebody deliberately put them in the wastebasket!"

"Oh, Nancy, that is preposterous!" Mrs. Corning said. "Who would do that?"

"Someone who's trying to sabotage the seventy-fifth anniversary library celebration, that's who!" I said. I looked straight at Mrs. Corning. "I don't suppose you'd know what Mr. Franklin was doing yesterday afternoon between four and six o'clock?"

"Well, as a matter of fact I do. He was doing some yard work for me—for which I pay him very well, if you're thinking that I ask my employees to do personal things without compensation," Mrs. Corning said. She stood up. "Nancy, I've never known you to blame other people for your mistakes, but if this celebration is to succeed, then you'll just have to be more careful about what you do." Mrs. Corning turned and started back to her desk. "Now, if you'll excuse me, there are other things going on in the library that I simply must take care of."

I knew I had to get out of there before I said some things that I would regret later. I couldn't believe that the very person who had asked me to chair the library decoration committee and to help find the missing library clock had now turned against me. Someone had deliberately set out not only to scuttle the library celebration, but to destroy my reputation at the same time, and I was determined to find out who it was.

I led the way out of Mrs. Corning's office, with Bess and George right behind me—but instead of stopping at my desk, I headed toward the opposite side of the reference stacks, where I knew there were some secluded tables. I had to think, and I didn't want anybody else around right now except Bess and George.

"What was that all about?" Bess said, as the three of us sat down.

I shrugged. "My head's still swimming from all the accusations that have been hurled at me," I said. "I'm trying to put it all together."

"I don't think any of this is just a coincidence, Nancy," George said. "Somebody is behind it."

"Oh, I agree, George—and now I have to find out who," I said.

"Well, just start naming names, Nancy," Bess suggested, "and then you can see who would have the best motive."

"Mr. Franklin has moved back to the top of my list, because of what happened to the essays," I said.

"That makes sense, but why did you want to know where he was yesterday afternoon?" Bess asked.

I told them about how Ned and I had driven by both the Mullins and Franklin houses. "It occurred to me that they might have planned to steal the library clock together," I said. I elaborated on my theory. "They may not have been meeting yesterday afternoon, like I thought at first, but that still doesn't mean they aren't in this thing together."

"That certainly makes sense," George said.

"That's what I thought too," I said.

Just then I looked up to see Ned striding our way. I could tell by the look on his face that he wasn't happy about something.

Since I didn't want anyone to remind me that we were in a library, I waited until he reached us to say anything.

"This is a surprise," I said. "What are you doing here?"

Ned gave me one of his looks. "I called your house and Hannah said you'd just left, so I left you a message here that I'd be right over," he said. "I just wanted to see how things are going for you. I don't know which librarian I talked to, but whoever answered your phone said she'd tell you or leave you a note."

"I'm sorry, Ned," I said. "I didn't check my desk." I looked at Bess and George. "But that's exactly what I'm going to do now."

The three of them followed me over to my desk, which was secluded from the other reference librarian by a couple of bookcases. I probably wouldn't have been so lucky, but the library was in the process of hiring another reference librarian, so this desk was available.

No message.

"You don't know who you talked to?" I asked Ned.

Ned shook his head. "I didn't ask, and the person didn't tell me, but you know something—now that I think about it, the voice sounded kind of familiar."

"Really?" Bess said.

Ned nodded. "But we didn't talk long enough for me to place it," he added.

I told Ned about the missing recollections. "Of course, people will sometimes tell you they'll leave a note for the person you're calling, and they never get around to doing it," I added. "But with all the other things happening, it just seems like part of a pattern."

"Agreed," George said.

"What do you want to do now, Nancy?" Bess said. "I don't want to hurry you, but there are some other things I need to do this morning."

I let out a big sigh. "I don't think there's anything that we can do," I said. "This whole project just seems to be collapsing around me. I've never really felt like this before."

"I know it's frustrating, Nancy," Ned said encouragingly, "but you can't give up."

"Oh, I won't give up, Ned," I said. "You know me

better than that!" I snapped my fingers. "In fact, this might be a good time to check in with Chief McGinnis."

"What for?" George cried.

"It would just be a waste of time," Bess added.

"Well, I should keep him up to date on whatever I found," I said. I at least like to *try* to have a good relationship with the River Heights chief of police.

"You know that he'll just try to pick your brain, Nancy," George said, "and then he'll take all the credit for your hard work."

"There's not a whole lot left to pick, George," I said. "Anyway, as long as the mystery gets solved, then that's the main thing. I'm not looking for glory."

I asked Bess if she'd drive my car to her house, and told her that I'd pick it up later. That way, Ned and I could go together to Chief McGinnis's office.

"That'd be great," Bess said. "That'll give me a chance to take a look under the hood. On the way over here, I heard a pinging noise, and it has me concerned."

"Well, just make sure it's put back together before I need it again," I said.

Bess held up her hands. "Have I ever failed you before?" she said.

I grinned. "No, never," I agreed.

After Bess and George left, I suddenly remembered that I needed to address some envelopes to children's writers in the area. I had pulled their addresses off the Internet, and I planned to send them fliers about the celebration, with a note asking them if they'd like to attend as a special guest of the Mahoney Library.

"Sorry, Ned," I said.

"No problem, Nancy. I'll just look around at the different collections," Ned said. "This place has always fascinated me."

It didn't take me long to get through the addressing, and I collected Ned. As we were pulling out of the library parking lot, I saw Deirdre getting into her car. Where had *she* been?

When we got to police headquarters, we found Chief McGinnis in the snack room, his mouth full of jelly doughnut. He held up a box with only one left. "Want it?" he asked.

I shook my head. "I never, never take a person's last doughnut, Chief," I said. "It's a creed I live by!"

Well, that joke totally went over his head. I could tell that Ned was trying not to laugh—whether at the chief or the joke, I wasn't sure.

Chief McGinnis wiped the sugar off his face with the back of his hand, and said, "If you want information about the library clock theft, then I have to—"

I shook my head. "No, no," I said, interrupting him. "I'm here to fill you in on what I know so far."

Chief McGinnis stood up quickly. "Oh, well, that's a different story altogether," he said. "Come on down to my office, and you can tell me what you've found out, so . . ." He stopped. I was sure he had suddenly realized that he was looking way too eager to get information on the case, so he redirected his sentence with, "Well, it's probably stuff we already know."

"I know, I know, it probably is," I said, humoring him.

When we finally got to Chief McGinnis's office, Ned and I sat in the two chairs in front of his desk. Chief McGinnis turned on a tape recorder, gave the date and the time, then said, "Please state your name and address."

I went along with the charade. We've been doing this for years: I get recorded, he takes the credit!

"Now, Ms. Drew, please tell me what information you have that relates to the theft of the library clock," Chief McGinnis said.

At that moment I had a thought. I decided only to tell Chief McGinnis my suspicions about Ralph Mullins—how I thought he might have stolen the clock himself so he could sell it. "He's a locksmith at the university," I said. "He could have figured out a way to get into the library when nobody was inside."

When I finished talking about Ralph Mullins, I stopped. Chief McGinnis looked at me for several seconds, but he didn't stop the tape recorder. "Go on," he finally said.

"That's it," I said.

I knew Ned wouldn't prod me to add anything about Willy Franklin. I had decided that it might be better if I just presented Chief McGinnis one suspect at a time, and right now, Ralph Mullins seemed a stronger suspect than Willy Franklin.

Chief McGinnis narrowed his eyes at me. "Are you sure?" he said.

"Yes, I'm sure," I told him. "What's wrong? Don't you think this is good information?"

"Now really," Chief McGinnis said. "Ralph Mullins is one of our suspects too. He's had several run-ins with the law, so naturally he was at the top of my list. In fact, we have a tail on him. We know his every move."

I shrugged. "I'm sorry," I said. "I'll keep digging too, and maybe I can come up with something else."

Chief McGinnis stood up. "Well, I can't stop you—but just make sure you let me know what you find out, because if you don't, then it's probably obstruction of justice."

Just then my cell phone went off. I recognized our home telephone number. That usually means Hannah needs something from the grocery store. I figured I'd call her after we left Chief McGinnis's office.

"Shouldn't you take that?" Chief McGinnis said. "It could be something important."

I shook my head. "Sorry," I said. "It's just Hannah. She probably needs something from the market. I'll call her in a minute." I stood up. "Well, thank you for your time. I'll certainly let you know when I find out something else."

Chief McGinnis stood up, and Ned and I left the office.

As we headed down the steps in front of the building, Ned said, "There's no way they have a tail on Ralph Mullins. We would have noticed it."

"Well, that's why we came, Ned," I said. "They'll have a tail on him now."

"Ha! Nice work, Nancy!" Ned said. "That's what you wanted all along—for Chief McGinnis to put a tail on him. If you had asked him directly, he wouldn't have done it."

"Exactly," I told him. "If I had told him about Willy Franklin, he might have put a tail on him, too. But at this point, I want Chief McGinnis to focus on Ralph Mullins." I punched redial on my cell phone to see what Hannah wanted. When she answered, I said, "Market stop?"

"No, not this time, Nancy," Hannah said. "You had a telephone call from a Mr. Henry Mead a few minutes ago. He said he had some information for you about the theft of the library clock."

7

Just Like an Old Case

That's odd, I thought. "Did he leave a number where he could be reached?" I asked Hannah.

"No. He just said he wanted to talk to you in person, Nancy," Hannah said. "He gave me his address with directions on how to get there."

"Just a minute," I said. I quickly took a notepad out of my purse. "Go ahead," I told Hannah. I recognized the address right away. Henry Mead lives in one of the new estates with multimillion-dollar homes being built along the Muskoka River north of River Heights. They all have French names, and each estate is the size of three normal houses put together. "Thanks, Hannah," I said.

"What's up?" Ned asked.

I told him about the message, then asked if he'd like to join me.

"Sure," Ned replied. "Who is this guy, anyway?"

"He's a friend of the family. He and Dad roomed together in college," I said. "He is a lawyer who specializes in wills and trusts."

"Sounds promising," Ned said.

Ned and I got back into his car and headed for the highway that would take us to Mr. Mead's house. It paralleled the river, so it was a beautiful drive.

It took us half an hour to get to the estates, then another fifteen minutes to find Mr. Mead's address. This was the first time I had ever been in this particular development, and I was absolutely stunned by how huge the homes were.

There were several expensive cars parked in the long driveway that led to Mr. Mead's house.

"Did Hannah say anything about a party?" Ned asked. "Is that why we're here?"

"No, she just said that Mr. Mead wanted to talk to me right away," I replied.

"Where should I park, Nancy?" Ned asked.

I looked around, trying to spot an open space near the front entrance. There was none, so I said, "Just pull up near the front door and wait. I'll go find out what he wants me to know, and if it's going to take more than a few minutes, I'll call you on your cell phone. Okay?"

"Okay," Ned said.

When Ned drove under the portico, I hopped out, ran up the marble steps, and rang the bell. Almost immediatcly the door opened, and a man dressed like a butler said, "Yes?"

"I'm Nancy Drew," I told him. "Mr. Mead called and wanted me to come by. He said he had some information for me about the library clock that was stolen."

I could tell by the look on the man's face that he didn't know what I was talking about.

"Well, I'm sorry, Miss Drew, but I honestly don't think . . ."

Just then I looked over the man's shoulder and saw Henry Mead talking to a couple who looked as though they were about to leave.

"Mr. Mead!" I called to him.

The butler looked aghast. "Miss Drew, *please!* This isn't the time to—"

"Is that Nancy Drew?" Mr. Mead called. He motioned to the couple that he'd be right back, then he headed toward the front door. "Well, this is a very pleasant surprise," he said when he reached me.

The butler, realizing now that I wasn't some party crasher, did an expert disappearing act.

"I'm sorry to interrupt your party," I said, "but your call sounded so urgent."

"My call?" Mr. Mead said.

I told him the message Hannah had relayed to me.

"But, Nancy, I never made that telephone call," Mr. Mead said.

"You didn't?" I said.

"No. In fact, I have to tell you that I honestly didn't know about the disappearance of the library clock," Mr. Mead said. "I just returned from the Caribbean last night. Some of my law firm partners planned this surprise celebration for me." He leaned over so he could whisper. "I landed a really big account." He grinned. "Their incomes just tripled! They're having a good time thanking me for it."

"Congratulations," I said.

He sighed. "Actually, I envy your father. Criminal law is much more exciting," he said. "Sometimes, I wish that I had—oh, I don't want to bore you, Nancy. I'm sorry. In any case, I can't imagine who would call you and say that it was me. It's a mystery—but then, that's your specialty, isn't it?" He winked.

"Yes, I guess it is!" I said. "I'd better go. My friend Ned's waiting for me. It was good to see you—and congratulations again."

"Give my best to your father," Mr. Mead said. "I

need to call him soon. We don't see enough of each other."

"He'd like that, I'm sure," I said.

The butler magically reappeared at the front door and let me out.

"Well?" Ned said when I got inside his car. "Did you learn anything important?"

I nodded. "Somebody has played another dirty trick on me," I said. "That's what I learned."

"What do you mean?" Ned asked as he turned around and headed back down the driveway.

I told him everything that Mr. Mead had said.

Ned shook his head. "Who would want to send you on a wild-goose chase like this?" he said.

I thought for a moment.

"Maybe they didn't," I said. "It could be a clue."

Ned looked at me. "What do you mean?" he asked.

"Henry Mead's specialty is wills and trusts," I told him. "The mystery of the library clock is all about wills and trusts. Ned, maybe somebody is trying to tell me something."

All the way back to River Heights, I tried to figure out just where the telephone call fit as far as the mystery was concerned. I didn't have much luck. As usual, Ned drove and left me alone with my thoughts.

When he finally pulled up in front of my house, I

saw that Bess had returned my car—and I was so glad, because I was too tired to go get it. "I'm sorry I wasted your time, Ned," I said. "I hope you still have time to get some work done at the library."

"I'm fine, Nancy," Ned said. "You're the one I'm concerned about."

"It's okay, Ned. I know it'll all come together," I said.

"I'll call you later, okay?" Ned said.

"Okay."

That night after dinner I had another talk with Dad. He thought the phone call from the Henry Mead imposter was odd too, and he didn't have an explanation for it. He agreed with me, though, that there had to be some connection here to the disappearance of the library clock.

"I think that either Mr. Franklin or Mr. Mullins, or both of them together, stole the library clock. And I'm beginning to think, after that telephone call, that there might be more people involved with it," I said. "Plus, I'm almost positive that Deirdre Shannon is behind all the problems with the library celebration."

"Do you have any *real* evidence to support your claims, Nancy?" Dad asked me.

"No," I said, "but it all makes sense."

"Well, Nancy, I think you're on track with the

library clock, because what you've uncovered up to this point does seem to lead to the possibility of one or both of those men being involved," he said. "But I honestly don't see that kind of evidence with the library celebration problems. As you know, you have to have hard evidence," Dad continued. "I know that you and Deirdre don't like each other, and frankly, it's easy to see why, but that doesn't necessarily translate into her being responsible for these problems at the library. If you think about it objectively, it could all just be a series of unfortunate coincidences."

"I know you're right, Dad, and I'll try to keep that in mind," I said. "It just seems odd to me that whenever I discover something else that's gone wrong with the celebration, Deirdre is always around."

"Well, you told me she's on your committee," Dad said, "so she does have a reason for being at the library at the same time you are."

He had a point there. I've heard his lecture many times about how you have to avoid speculation and look for solid evidence if you want to win a case.

The next morning, just as I was getting out of bed, the telephone on my night stand rang. It was Ned.

"Listen, Nancy, I have a big favor to ask of you," Ned said. "One of the copyeditors is sick today, so I'm down at the newspaper, helping Dad. But I couldn't get my car started this morning, so I had to come with him. Could you take me to the library in about thirty minutes, so I can meet with my study group?"

"Sure, Ned," I told him. "That won't be a problem."

I jumped out of bed, ran to the bathroom, turned on the steaming shower jets, and allowed the hot water to wake me up. After I toweled off, I used the blow dryer on my hair, and then grabbed some clothes from my closet. A quick glance at the clock on my nightstand told me I was already running late. I dabbed on a little eye shadow, yelled good-bye to Hannah, and was out the door.

Ten minutes later I arrived in front of the *River Heights Bugle*. Ned wasn't standing outside as he had promised, so I found a parking space two stores down and pulled in.

Just as I got out of the car and shut the door, I realized that my keys were still in the ignition. And the doors lock automatically.

I try never to panic about anything, because this is not a quality admired in detectives, but the real reason I wasn't worried is because I have a very good friend with the road emergency service I belong to, Charlie Adams. He drives a truck for one of the local garages, and he's always willing to drop whatever he's doing to come unlock my car door so I can retrieve my keys.

I pressed #12 on my cell phone autodial; I've forgotten my keys so many times I programmed Charlie's number in. He picked up on the third ring.

"Hi, Charlie, it's Nancy," I said. "I need—"

"Just give me the address," Charlie said, "and I'll be there in a second."

See, I told you this has happened more than once.

Within a few minutes he was at my car. "Where were you?" I asked, totally impressed by his speed.

"I was just two blocks over," Charlie said. He gave me one of his biggest smiles. "I'm glad I was close by, because I wouldn't want you to wait in this hot sun."

It didn't take Charlie long to open the door, using what looked like a flimsy ruler to me—and in that short time, he managed to fill me in on most of the River Heights gossip.

"But I saved the best for last, Nancy," Charlie said. He opened my car door, retrieved my keys, and handed them to me. "The Smalley family has moved back to River Heights. I saw Merrie and Carrie at the grocery store last night. They're just as—" His mouth suddenly dropped open. "There they are!"

I turned and looked. I felt my stomach drop. Merrie and Carrie Smalley were just going into Greene's Department Store across the street.

"I have to go, Charlie," I said. "I want to see what those two are up to."

"Okay, Nancy, I understand," Charlie said. "You've got a mystery to solve, right?"

"That's right!" I shouted over my shoulder. "Thanks again for opening my door."

If you're wondering why I didn't give Charlie any money for his work, it's because he wouldn't take it anyway. For years I would argue with him about it, but he insisted that it was up to him to decide if he needed to charge a customer for the work he did.

My mind turned back to Carrie and Merrie. Why in the world had the Smalleys moved back to River Heights? If there were two girls I disliked more than Deirdre Shannon, it was Merrie and Carrie. We also went to school together, and they tried to make my life miserable. Of course, they never succeeded—but I always felt as though I had to watch my back. Things had been bad between us forever, it seemed, because it was quite obvious they were jealous of me and my friends. But things went from bad to worse after I discovered that the bona fide will of a man named Albert Washington left the Smalley family nothing—after they thought they were getting *all* of his money!

What really concerned me now, though, was that the lawyer for the other Smalley relatives, the people who were contesting the will, was Henry Mead. This couldn't just be a coincidence. Right after the Smalleys were disinherited, they moved away from River Heights. Hearing that they were back in town now really bothered me. I knew they would not have forgotten my role in their legal troubles. And what I wanted to know is what they were up to now—and if it had anything to do with a missing clock.

8

The Smalley Sisters Return

After making a quick call to Ned, letting him know I'd be late—he was used to this—I headed toward the front entrance to Greene's Department Store. My brain kept trying out reasons why the Smalleys had moved back to River Heights. It was just so unusual. When I pulled open the door, I immediately saw Merrie and Carrie. They were halfway down the wide main aisle of the store. They were laughing about something. Suddenly Merrie gestured dramatically, and her arm struck a large ceramic vase, knocking it to the floor.

A salesclerk on the other side of the display hurried over to them and surveyed the damage.

I was close enough to hear her say, "Oh, ma'am, this is terrible. That vase cost five hundred dollars!

You'll need to talk to the manager about what happened."

"What for?" Merrie said. "I'm certainly not going to pay for it, if that's what you're getting at!"

"Do you work in this department?" Carrie demanded.

"Why, yes, I do," the salesclerk said.

"Are you responsible for how the vases are arranged in this display?" Carrie asked.

"Yes, I unpack them and put them on the table," the salesclerk said. "Why do you ask?"

"Well, isn't it obvious?" Merrie said.

"You're the reason the vase fell off the table!" Carrie shouted at her.

I saw the salesclerk's face drop. "What do you mean?" she said. "There's no way that it's my—"

Just then another woman, who I knew was the manager of this department, walked up to the three of them.

"What's the problem, Mary?" the woman asked the salesclerk.

Before the salesclerk could reply, Carrie said, "Your employee accused my sister of breaking this vase. It is obvious to us that she put it too close to the table edge. You should take the cost of the vase out of her salary."

The salesclerk turned to the manager. "I'm sure it

83

wasn't too close to the edge," she said. "I never . . ."

Well, there was no way I was going to let these two creepy Smalley sisters turn the tables on this poor girl, so I hurried up to them and said, "I saw the whole thing! It wasn't your salesclerk's fault at all." I looked at Merrie. "You weren't watching what you were doing, Ms. Smalley. You shouldn't gesture so dramatically near a table with breakable items."

"Oh, thank you, thank you," the salesclerk said. "I knew that I hadn't put that vase too close to the edge of the display table."

"Thank you, Ms. . . . Oh, I know you," the manager said. "You're Nancy Drew!"

"She most certainly is!" Merrie snarled.

Carrie glared at me.

Shoot. The dogs were loose!

"Well, thank you again, Ms. Drew," the manager said, turning to the salesclerk. "Get the custodian to clean this up, Mary. We certainly don't want anyone to get hurt. And I will expect you two girls"—she looked at the Smalleys—"to pay for the damage in due time."

"Yes, ma'am," the salesclerk said.

The Smalley sisters snarled at each other. Clearly this was not the way they thought their shopping trip would turn out.

Now I was alone with the Smalley twins, and I felt

as though the temperature had suddenly plunged to below freezing. But I was determined to try and find out as much as I could from them.

"I hear that you and your family are thinking about moving back to River Heights," I said.

Merrie and Carrie looked at each other and smirked.

"Yes, if everything works out as planned—and I certainly see no reason why it won't," Merrie said.

"We'll once again be residents of this fair city!" Carrie shrieked.

I felt a chill run through me. "Didn't you like where you were living?" I asked.

"No!" Carrie almost shouted at me. "This was our home, and we didn't want to leave. Your meddling forced us to."

"You'll be sorry for what you did to us!" Merrie added, menacingly.

With that, the two of them turned sharply and stormed out of the store.

I just stood there, stunned, trying to imagine my life in River Heights with Merrie and Carrie Smalley scheming to find ways to get even with me.

I waited for a couple of minutes, just to make sure the Smalley twins had disappeared from sight, then I left the department store myself and headed back toward the *River Heights Bugle*.

Ned was sitting on the hood of my car when I got there. He had a bemused expression on his face.

"Oh, Ned, I'm so sorry. Something came up," I shouted to him.

"I know," Ned said. "Charlie told me."

"This is probably one of the worst days of my life," I said. "I was so happy when Merrie and Carrie moved. It was like a terrible gloom had lifted from over River Heights."

"I'm just as disappointed as you are to hear this news," Ned said, hopping down off the hood. "The Smalleys are such unpleasant people."

I told Ned what the twins had said before they left. "I don't know what to think, Ned," I said. "You'll probably think I'm just being paranoid, but now I believe that they're somehow involved in everything that's going on."

"Well, I really do believe that's a stretch, Nancy," Ned observed. "You have to admit that you can't be very objective where the Smalley twins are concerned."

"Yes, I admit that, I really do, but . . . ," I started to say, then I threw up my hands. "Oh, I don't want to think about them now." I looked at my watch and let out a big sigh. "I'm late for a library committee meeting."

"Did I know about this one?" Ned asked.

I let out a big sigh. "I guess I forgot to mention it," I said.

"Why don't you just cancel it and we'll go get some comfort food, like an ice-cream sundae?" Ned said.

"It's tempting, Ned—but I'm already so far behind with my plans, that I may never catch up," I said. "I'd rather explain why we're late than explain why I just canceled the whole meeting." I stopped and looked at him. "Oh, Ned! I was supposed to take you to the library, so you could meet with your study group," I said. "I'm so sorry! Why didn't you mention that when I got back?"

"Well, I knew how traumatic finding out about the Smalley twins would be for you, so I called one of the guys in the group on my cell phone, and told him I wouldn't be there," Ned said. "I'm basically just tutoring everybody when I go, anyway; this will force them to do a little digging on their own. It's no big deal."

I gave him a peck on the cheek. "You are the sweetest thing," I said, "and I'm the biggest dope."

Ned took me by the shoulders. "You are not a dope," he said. "You're Nancy Drew, and you've got a mystery to solve, so quit feeling sorry for yourself!"

"That is a little out of character for me, isn't it?" I said with a grin.

"I'll say it is," Ned said.

"Come on," I said, getting into my car. "Let's go to the library, and get this case cracked."

When Ned and I entered the library, I knew at once that something else was wrong. You know how you see people huddled together in a little group, and then when they see you approaching, they look all guilty—like they're just sure you know they're talking about you? And they are, but they try to look all innocent. Well, that's what the librarians looked like.

It was almost funny. I say *almost* because I wasn't laughing. I was starting to have another one of those sick feelings in the pit of my stomach.

"Get ready," Ned whispered to me. "You may have to face the music sooner than you thought you would."

Just then all the librarians started off in different directions, leaving the center of their huddle standing there: Mrs. Corning. She was giving me a steely look. I couldn't imagine what had happened now.

"I'm sorry I'm late," I called to her, not really caring that she might tell me to remember that I was in a library and that I shouldn't talk so loud. I could see no other patrons nearby, so I doubted I would be disturbing anyone. "Something came up. I guess the rest of the committee left."

Mrs. Corning nodded, but she still didn't say anything.

When Ned and I reached her, I said, "Is there anything wrong?"

"Well, I'll give you two guesses, and the first one doesn't count," Mrs. Corning said.

I almost laughed. I hadn't heard that line since elementary school, and even then it was from one of my classmates, not from an adult.

"I'm sorry, Mrs. Corning," I said. "I honestly don't feel like playing guessing games."

"Well, Nancy, that's the problem," Mrs. Corning said. "This celebration isn't a game."

"I wasn't talking about the celebration, Mrs. Corning," I said. Now I was beginning to get angry. I was tired of whoever it was creating problems for me. "I was talking about what was wrong."

At that moment another one of the librarians came up and stood beside Mrs. Corning. She was holding the stack of envelopes that I had addressed to area children's writers.

Mrs. Corning nodded at the stack of envelopes. "Martha found these in the bottom drawer of the filing cabinet next to your desk," she said. "They were supposed to have gone out by yesterday."

"I know. That's why I put them in the outbox on

89

my desk," I said. "I have no idea who put them in the filing cabinet."

"Perhaps you just *think* you put them in the out-box," Mrs. Corning said. "You've been rather distracted lately, and things like this happen when people get distracted."

I thought for a minute, while everyone just stared at me. "Wait a minute," I said. "What made Martha look in that bottom drawer?"

"Deirdre suggested it," Martha said.

I looked at Ned. "Really?" I said. "That's very interesting. I wonder what made her think of having you do that?"

"She was here for the committee meeting this morning—*on time,*" Mrs. Corning said. "When you didn't show up, she asked me if I had a list of the authors you had invited, and I said no, that the invitations had already been sent out. But I told her there might be a list on your desk or in your filing cabinet, so I gave her permission to look."

"Why did she need to know that?" I demanded.

"She wanted to pull some of the books off the shelves to start the displays, that's why," Mrs. Corning said. "After all, nothing has really been done yet. I thought it was a very good idea."

"Of course," I said. "I wasn't thinking."

Actually, I *was* thinking. I was thinking that I had

been right all along. Deirdre Shannon was behind all the problems I was having with the library celebration. In fact, it didn't take too much effort to picture Deirdre sneaking into the library at night and prying the clock out of the wall, but I realized that that was probably ridiculous. Making my life miserable by sabotaging the efforts of my committee wasn't at all ridiculous.

I reached for the envelopes. "I'll go mail them now," I said.

"Oh, no, that's all right," Mrs. Corning said. "I'll take care of that myself."

I gritted my teeth. I had to keep my composure, something I was finding very difficult to do. "Fine," I said. I looked around. "I think I'll get Mr. Franklin to move some of the display cases. I have some ideas about where I want to put the books of area children's authors."

"Mr. Franklin quit this morning," Mrs. Corning said.

"He *quit*?" I said.

Mrs. Corning nodded. She looked at Ned. "I was hoping that your friend would be able to help you move the display cases."

"I can do that," Ned said hurriedly. He looked at me. "It's no problem, Nancy—and what I can't move by myself, I can get some friends to help me with."

I was hearing Ned, but not much of it was registering. I was on a mental roller coaster. "Does Mr. Franklin have another job?" I asked.

"He told me that he didn't, but he was wearing brand-new clothes," Mrs. Corning said. "That seemed kind of odd to me."

Odd, indeed. If you quit a job, you didn't go and buy new clothes—unless, of course, you came into a lot of money from selling an old clock!

"Nancy! There you are!"

I turned to see Ellis heading in our direction. He had a big smile on his face, and he was looking only at me.

When he reached us, he said, "I'd love to go with you to the movies tonight."

I blinked. "What?" I said. I could feel Ned looking at me.

"I said, I'd love to go with you to the movies tonight," Ellis repeated. He was totally oblivious to Ned's standing beside me. "What time do you want me to pick you up?"

"What are you talking about, Ellis?" I finally managed to say. "I don't know anything about this."

Now it was Ellis's turn to look puzzled. "You left a message on my answering machine, asking me if I wanted to go to the movies tonight," Ellis said. "You must have called when I was in the shower."

"It wasn't me, Ellis," I said.

"Well, it certainly sounded like your voice," Ellis countered. "You said, 'This is Nancy. Let's go to the movies tonight. There's something important I have to discuss with you.'"

I couldn't think of anything else to do but just stare at him. I had to face facts. These weren't just harmless pranks. Somebody in River Heights was out to destroy me!

9

Searching for Evidence

Fortunately for me, Ned seemed to believe my side of the story. But after the incident with Ellis, I just wanted to be alone. I had to escape from everything. So I dropped Ned off at his house, and then I drove home.

As soon as I opened the front door, the smell of Hannah's freshly baked cookies greeted me. I knew everything would be all right—at least for a while.

"I'm home, Hannah," I called to her.

Before I got to the kitchen, Hannah came out to meet me. She was drying her hands on a dish towel.

"What's wrong?" she asked.

Hannah can always tell by the tone of my voice when things aren't going right. Frankly I thought I had done a really good job of sounding cheery, trying to hide how I was truly feeling, but I should have known better than to try to fool her.

"It's a long story," I said.

"Well, I've got time for it," Hannah said. "You go on up to your room, take your shoes off, lie down on your bed, and I'll bring you up some cookies and milk."

I wanted to remind Hannah that I was probably a little old for this, but the whole idea sounded so perfect, that I did what she told me to do.

For the next hour it was like it had been in the years just after my mother's death, when Hannah had first come to live with us and take care of the house. She did so much more than she was hired to do. When I had any sort of problem, she'd listen, then add some of her wisdom—and I'd feel better. Of course, the cookies and milk probably helped a lot too, just as they were doing now.

"Nobody said solving mysteries is easy, Nancy," Hannah said. "If it were, then anybody could do it. You just need to free your mind of everything that's inside, then put it all back in a different order."

I didn't tell Hannah that that was easier said than done, because that would just sound like another excuse, so I tried to perk up a little. "I'll give it the old Nancy Drew try."

Hannah got up from the side of my bed. "You've

never failed to solve a case yet," she said, "so I know you'll be successful this time too."

Just then the doorbell rang.

When I started to get up, Hannah said, "I'll get it, Nancy. I need to get back to the kitchen anyway. It's probably one of the neighborhood kids delivering some of the things I bought last week."

"You're a soft touch, Hannah," I said.

Our pantry shelves were stacked with scented candles, unopened boxes of stationery, and tins of candy and nuts. We could probably have our own fund drive and make a lot of money off the things Hannah has bought from other people to help them raise money.

Hannah grinned back. "Maybe, but I like helping out the schools—and I admire the business know-how of these elementary-grade kids."

I snuggled into my pillow, enjoying the security of my bed, and began to sort out all the bits and pieces about the missing clock and the library celebration.

I was thinking about all of this when there was a soft knock on my door.

"Come in, Hannah," I said. "Show me what you bought."

"It's me," Ned said. "Are you decent?"

"Ned?" I sat up. "What are you doing here?"

"I just wanted to apologize," Ned said. "Are you decent?"

I got up from my bed, straightened the covers, and said, "Yes, it's fine. Come on in."

There are some comfortable chairs in front of a television set in one corner of my room, so I headed there, just as Ned came inside.

"What did you do that you need to apologize for?" I said, as I plopped down on a chair and put my feet on a stool. "I must have missed something."

Ned came over and sat down beside me. "I didn't mean to act so jealous when Ellis said he'd be glad to go with you to the movies tonight," Ned said. "I should have known somebody was playing a prank on him."

"Oh, Ned, I guess I didn't even notice," I said. "I'm sorry." I looked at him and grinned. "Were you jealous?" I said.

"Well, of course . . . ," Ned started to say, but the front doorbell rang again.

"This place is beginning to be like Grand Central Station," I said. "Now, *that* must be the neighborhood kids bringing Hannah whatever it is she ordered from them."

But it wasn't. Within seconds Bess and George bounded into my room.

"Oh, sorry," Bess said. "Hannah didn't tell us you had company."

"Ned was just apologizing to me for being jealous," I said, grinning. "I was trying to decide whether to accept his apology or not."

Ned grinned back. He stood up. "Well, call me when you've made your decision, Nancy Drew," he said. "I have to go to the university. See you later."

"Okay, Ned," I said.

When Ned was gone, Bess said, "Don't you feel well?"

I let out a big sigh. "I'm just frustrated, that's all," I said. "I can't seem to do anything right anymore."

"So, in other words, you're feeling sorry for yourself?" George said.

I rolled my eyes. "No, George, I'm not feeling sorry for myself," I said. "I'm just feeling . . . well, *incompetent*."

"Did it ever occur to you that that is exactly what these people want you to feel?" Bess said.

I looked at her. "What do you mean?" I asked.

"Nancy, even I can see what's happening," Bess said. "Whoever is behind this is playing mind games with you. They want you to give up."

"Do you really think so?" I said.

"I think Bess is right, Nancy," George said. "We

came over here just to tell you that we know you can solve this mystery."

"And we're here to help you do whatever needs to be done," Bess added.

"Thanks. I couldn't ask for two better friends," I said. "In fact, I'm already feeling better."

"Okay, so where do we start?" George said.

"Well, I'm not quite sure I need your help right this minute with the mystery, but just knowing that you haven't given up on me helps. I could sure use your help to make some posters to advertise the celebration, though," I said.

"Done!" George said.

I filled them in on what Mrs. Corning had told me about Mr. Franklin that morning. "I'm even more suspicious of him now than I was at first," I said.

"That *is* odd," Bess agreed. "If you quit your job, you don't go right out and buy new clothes."

"Well, I certainly wouldn't," George said. "He's either really dumb, or he's come into some money."

"I don't think he's dumb," I told them. I picked up the telephone. "I just thought of a plan. I'm going to call Chief McGinnis."

Of course, both Bess and George thought I was crazy, but I knew what I had in mind would work better if he were involved. I called him and asked him if he could come by for me, because I had something I needed to talk to him about: Willy Franklin. He agreed, reluctantly—but I could tell in his voice that he wanted to find out if I had discovered something new about the mystery. Of course, knowing how little he does, I was sure that anything I had found out would be more than he had.

By the time Chief McGinnis arrived, Bess and George had already left. I ran outside to his patrol car.

"Let's go for a drive," I said.

"I'm not supposed to drive citizens around town, Nancy," Chief McGinnis said. "There's a city ordinance against it."

"It's not like you're taking me shopping, Chief McGinnis," I said, getting into the passenger side of the patrol car. "We're on a case."

Chief McGinnis hesitated. I could tell that he wanted to do something to exercise his authority in the situation, but he evidently couldn't think of anything.

He let out a big sigh and started backing out of our driveway. "Okay, Nancy," he said, "where are we going?"

"Willy Franklin's house," I said. I gave him the address, and told him what Mrs. Corning had said that morning.

"There could be all kinds of reasons why he

bought new clothes," Chief McGinnis said. "Maybe he had been saving up his money, and just decided to spend some of it to celebrate quitting his job."

I thought about that for a minute. "I suppose," I said, "but somehow he just doesn't seem the type to do something like that." I knew that wasn't much of an argument, but I just had a gut feeling about all this, and sometimes, when you're solving a mystery, you have to rely on that. "I still think we need to check him out. To me Willy Franklin doesn't seem the type to save up his salary. I think he must have come into some money recently. Maybe he stole the library clock and finally found somebody to buy it. That could account for a lot of money."

Chief McGinnis didn't say anything, but I could tell that he was thinking about what I had said.

We finally turned onto Willy Franklin's street, and Chief McGinnis parked the patrol car in front.

"Isn't this a little obvious?" I said. "I was thinking that we could park down the street, then come up through the alley, and see if we find anything suspicious."

Chief McGinnis looked at me. "Why would we do that?" he asked.

"Well, if he's guilty and sees us, he might escape," I patiently explained.

"He's expecting us, Nancy," Chief McGinnis said.

I could tell by the triumphal look in his eyes that he thought he had outsmarted me this time.

"Oh, well then, parking in front is probably the best thing," I managed to say, knowing that I sounded like an idiot. "I didn't realize that you had already talked to him."

"I called him right after you called me," Chief McGinnis said, still enjoying himself. "I knew you'd want to go see him Nancy—I've seen you meddle in enough cases to know your methods! I told him that I had a few questions about the library clock that I wanted to ask him. He was very cooperative and told me to come on over."

"I just hope he's still here," I said.

Chief McGinnis looked at me. "What do you mean?" he asked.

"Well, if Willy Franklin did steal the clock, then you just gave yourself away," I said. "He's not dumb. You just let him know that he might be a suspect in the theft."

Chief McGinnis obviously hadn't thought about that. "Come on!" he shouted. "We need to stop him!"

He literally ran up to the house. If Willy Franklin hadn't been scared before, he'd probably be scared now. Chief McGinnis looked like a one-man SWAT team.

"Police!" Chief McGinnis shouted. "Open up!"

"You're going to scare him," I whispered. "You don't want to do that. If you'll just—"

Suddenly the front door opened, and a sleepy-eyed Willy Franklin said, "What's all the commotion out here?"

"Oh, hi, Mr. Franklin," I said brightly, before he could figure out what I was doing there. "It's good to see you again. I'm sorry you won't be around to help with the library celebration!"

Mr. Franklin grunted. He turned to Chief McGinnis. "What did you want to talk to me about?" he asked.

"We need your help," I said. "Do you mind if we come in to talk?"

Chief McGinnis gave me a dirty look, but he didn't say anything.

"Oh, okay," Mr. Franklin said.

I think he was taken off guard by what I had just said. He was probably all set to have us accuse him of doing something wrong. He turned around, and we followed him into his living room. It wasn't as bad as I had thought it would be, but if he had stolen the library clock and sold it for a lot of money, then he hadn't spent any of it on furnishing his house.

"Have a seat," Mr. Franklin said.

I pushed aside some old newspapers and dirty clothes and sat down on the edge of the sofa. I was just hoping that some strange creature wouldn't crawl out from under one of the cushions.

"How can I help you?" Mr. Franklin said.

Yes! He'd really taken the bait. Before Chief McGinnis could mess up the investigation, I said, "I don't know why we didn't think of this sooner, but you are probably the one person who can actually solve the mystery."

I could tell that Mr. Franklin didn't know what to say.

"You were in a position to see all the people who looked at the library clock," I continued, hoping to convince him that he really could be a help to the investigation, "so we thought we'd ask you to try and remember if you ever saw anybody who kept looking and looking at the clock, as though he—*or she*— were trying to figure out how to remove it from the wall."

Good grief. This was beginning to sound so dumb!

But Mr. Franklin already had the hook in his mouth. He started nodding his head, as though he was suddenly remembering all kinds of suspicious things that had taken place in the library. A smile came to his face, the first one I ever remembered seeing. I just knew that he was probably thinking that Chief McGinnis and I weren't very bright, and that

10

A Suspect Leaves Town

I quickly headed down the hall toward the door at the end. When I touched the knob to open it, it felt greasy, as though the last person who'd used it hadn't washed his hands after eating. Yuck.

Unfortunately I needed to look inside the room. Wrapping my hand in the bottom of my shirt, I reached out, turned the knob, and opened the door. The room looked like a bedroom, but it was piled so high with boxes and junk that it was hard to tell. I shut the door behind me and turned on the light. Carefully I wove my way through the clutter, hoping I would see the familiar library clock—but I could hardly find anything interesting, digging through stacks of dirty clothes and rummaging through some of the larger boxes.

I was hoping that Mr. Franklin was so engrossed in telling Chief McGinnis his theories about the robbery that he wouldn't be paying any attention to how long I was gone—but I knew I needed to hurry, just in case.

I turned off the light, stepped back into the hall, and looked in the three remaining rooms and the bathroom. They were all piled full of stuff too. What a way to live!

I started back down the hall, toward the living room. To my left I could see the kitchen, and I decided to check that out. In retrospect, I wished I hadn't. Dirty dishes were stacked everywhere. Hannah would absolutely pass out at the sight of it.

There was a door at the rear of the kitchen, and I was sure it led to the backyard. Then it occurred to me that there might be a shed where Mr. Franklin had hidden the clock. I peeked out one of the windows, and I didn't see any shed—plus, it was obvious that Mr. Franklin hadn't been in his yard for some time. Weeds had completely overtaken it. I suddenly wondered if he could have rented one of those storage facilities that have recently popped up all over River Heights. If he had done that, I'd either have to find the key, which he probably kept in his pocket, or follow him to the place and hope to get close enough to see him doing something with the clock.

I knew I had been gone way too long, so I quickly went back to the living room. I needn't have worried, though, because neither Chief McGinnis nor Mr. Franklin looked up when I sat down. It was as if I'd never left.

"I've seen that Lucy Gonsolvo looking at it too," Mr. Franklin was saying. "I remember once I almost had to carry her out of the library, because she wouldn't leave."

"Why is that?" I asked.

Mr. Franklin turned and looked at me. It took his eyes a couple of seconds to focus. It seemed he'd forgotten I was there. "She kept saying it reminded her of a clock she used to have back in the old country," he said. "That's what she called it, the *old country*— but she never did say where that was."

"I don't think anyone really knows where she's from," I said.

"So she could have taken the clock too," Mr. Franklin continued.

"Well, so far the list is up to fifteen possible suspects," Chief McGinnis said. "Can you think of anyone else?"

Mr. Franklin scratched his chin. "I'm sure there are others, but I can't rightly think of anyone else now. If I do, I'll give you a call. I want this clock to be back on the wall of the library as much as anyone else in

108

River Heights." He gave both of us a big smile.

Yeah, right. That wasn't the impression I'd gotten from him the other day. Of course, I didn't say that and chance making him angry. But I was positive that Mr. Franklin knew more about the clock than he was telling, and he was enjoying trying to throw us off the track by listing all the reasons other people in River Heights would have taken it.

I stood up. "Well, this has certainly been very helpful, Mr. Franklin, but we'd better be going."

Chief McGinnis gave me a look that said that he was in charge of this investigation, and that he should be the one to decide when to leave—even though he looked about as ready as I was. He'd probably try to pull rank on me once we got back into the patrol car too. I decided to make sure he had no reason to.

"I learned a lot about how to interrogate a suspect from you in there," I said as we headed to the patrol car. "That was like attending a course in criminal justice."

Chief McGinnis blinked. "Really?" he said.

I knew he was dying for me to elaborate, so I added, "Yes. It was quite obvious from the way you were just letting Mr. Franklin talk that the whole point was to get him to implicate himself."

"Why, yes, Nancy, that's exactly what my plan was," Chief McGinnis said. He cleared his throat. "It worked well, didn't it?"

I nodded. "A masterful stroke, really," I said. I could actually see his chest swelling. "It was all an attempt to throw us off the track, his implicating half the citizens of River Heights. In doing so, he made it quite clear that he knows more about the disappearance of the library clock than he wants us to believe."

"That's what I was thinking too," Chief McGinnis said. "I was hoping my plan would work."

"Oh, it did, Chief McGinnis," I said. "It did."

All the way back to my house, Chief McGinnis had a smile on his face. Just as he pulled into my driveway, I said, "I think you should put a man on him. If he goes to pick up the clock so he can sell it, you can pick him up."

"I'm one step ahead of you, Nancy," Chief McGinnis said. "I had already decided to do that."

"Great!" I told him.

I waved good-bye, then headed toward my front door. Hannah opened it just as I reached for the door-knob.

"Oh!" I cried. "You startled me!"

"Sorry, Nancy, I didn't mean to," Hannah said. "I saw you arrive, so I thought I'd let you in."

I suddenly realized that I had left the house without my purse and my keys. "Thanks, Hannah," I said. "Chief McGinnis picked me up so we could talk to

Mr. Franklin about the missing library clock. That's all that was on my mind."

"Oh, you got a telephone call from Lizzie Romer," Hannah said. "She sounded kind of frantic."

"Lizzie Romer?" I said. "Are you sure that's who it was?"

Hannah nodded. "She asked me to tell you that she really needs to talk to you, and could you meet her tomorrow for lunch at her sister Janice's apartment," she said. "I wrote down the address for you and put it in your room."

I couldn't believe it. Lizzie and Janice Romer were distant relatives of Albert Washington, the man whose third, handwritten will I'd found—the will that disinherited the Smalleys.

"Maybe I should call Lizzie right now," I said. "Did she leave her telephone number?"

"No, but she said she was leaving right away, and that she would be busy for the rest of the evening," Hannah said. "She didn't give me a cell phone number either; I don't know if she has one or not."

As I headed upstairs to my room, my head was spinning. It was bad enough that I had all the problems associated with the library celebration. Did an old case I had thought was solved need to start unraveling now?

★ ★ ★ ★

I didn't sleep well that night, and that's kind of unusual for me. I kept tossing and turning and trying to piece everything together. I may have gotten just a couple of hours' sleep. After thinking of all the reasons I didn't really want to get up the next morning, I finally thought of one that, although it didn't quite get me out of bed, at least made me sit up enough that I could reach the phone on the night table. I dialed Chief McGinnis's number.

"Hi, Chief McGinnis?" I said, after he'd said hello. "I just wanted to find out if your men had learned anything about Mr. Franklin."

I half expected a condescending reply, but he surprised me with, "Yes, Nancy, as a matter of fact, they did."

When he didn't elaborate, I said, "What?"

"He went to several clothing stores and bought some shirts and trousers, some socks, some underwear, a couple of belts, and some shoes."

Interesting. "Which stores?" I asked.

Chief McGinnis named some of the less expensive department stores in River Heights. "He didn't go anywhere else after that, except home," he added, "but I have a man in an unmarked car at the end of the block. If he leaves, we'll know about it."

I took that opportunity to tell Chief McGinnis that instead of going to get a glass of water the day before, I'd actually searched the house.

The change in his breathing told me that he wasn't happy with that bit of news, but he didn't complain. I was pretty sure that he wanted to know if I had found anything.

"I didn't find anything, though, no library clock, no clock parts," I said. "But Mr. Franklin could have simply rented one of those storage facilities and hidden it there."

I knew that Chief McGinnis had put his hand over the mouthpiece and was talking to someone in the office. It was muffled, but I could make out something about checking storage facilities. I wasn't sure how he planned to do that, because I didn't think we had enough cause for a court order to search any storage shed that Mr. Franklin might have rented. Maybe he was just going to find out if Mr. Franklin had rented one. That would be suspicious in itself—especially if it had happened within the last few days.

"I've got to go, Nancy," Chief McGinnis said, now talking into the phone again. "If I learn anything new, I'll get in touch with you."

I wouldn't hold my breath! "Okay," I said. " Same here."

Just as I hung up, I heard Hannah answering the front door downstairs. Within seconds Bess and George had bounded upstairs and into my room.

"Quick! Get dressed!" Bess said. "You're coming with us!"

"What's going on?" I asked.

"You won't believe what we just saw," George said.

"Okay," I said. I pulled on the clothes I had worn the previous night. "Ready!"

"Oh, Nancy. You're not going out like that, are you?" Bess said, staring at me. "Nothing matches."

I looked down. "Okay, I guess you're right," I said. I had forgotten that the chair where I tossed my clothes the night before also had some things on it from the night before that. They really didn't match—even I could see that. "Sorry." I quickly took off the clashing top and put on the matching top. "Better?" I asked.

Bess merely raised an eyebrow. It really wasn't that much better, I knew, but wasn't what they wanted to show me more important than my outfit?

Shaking her head, Bess led the way downstairs. We jumped into her car.

"Where are we going?" I asked.

"You'll see," George said.

"I feel like I'm being kidnapped," I said.

"Well, you may beg somebody to do just that after you see this," Bess said. "Keep watching on the right-hand side."

Three blocks later I let out a gasp. Through the window I saw one of the biggest mansions on River Street, and standing on the lawn, bossing around some movers, were Merrie and Carrie Smalley.

"You've got to be kidding me," I said, twisting my neck to watch out the rear window after we had passed them. "How in the world can the Smalleys afford a house like this?"

"Beats me," Bess said. "Man, I detest those two!"

I turned around. "I saw them in a store earlier, and they talked about how, if things went the way they hoped they would, they'd be moving back to River Heights soon."

"Well, it looks as though those 'things' went pretty well after all," George said. "Hmm. I wonder what 'things' they were talking about."

"That's what I want to know," I said.

"Do you want to drive past their house again?" Bess asked. "They were too busy bossing those movers to see us the first time."

"No, I'm not sure I want to risk them noticing us. They'll probably see us the second time, and I don't want to give them the satisfaction of thinking we care that much about their moving back to River Heights!" I said.

"I'm with you on that," George said. "I can't stand those two."

"I'm also supposed to have lunch with the Romer sisters. I need to get ready for that," I said.

"Romer, Romer," Bess said. "Why is that name familiar?"

I reminded them about the case I had worked on a while back that disinherited the Smalleys.

"Oh, that's odd," George said. "Do you think it's all connected?"

"I don't know *what* to think," I said, "but I'll call you when I get back from lunch."

When we got back to my house, Bess pulled in the driveway and let me out.

Just as I started to unlock the door, Hannah pulled it open. This was becoming a habit.

"You need to call Chief McGinnis right away," Hannah said.

I raced upstairs, so I could jot down any important information in the notebook I keep next to the telephone.

This time Chief McGinnis's secretary answered, but she recognized my voice and said, "Hold, please, Nancy."

When Chief McGinnis came on the line, he wasted no time. "Mr. Franklin took a taxi to the bus station. He bought a ticket to San Antonio, Texas. He only had one small suitcase with him," he said. "The officer who followed him there said he looked really scared about something."

11

The Puzzle Is Almost Complete

Something's not adding up here, Chief McGinnis,"
I said. "Mr. Franklin never struck me as a person who
would be afraid of anything."

"Now, why would my officer make up a thing like
that, Nancy?" Chief McGinnis said. "If she thought
the man looked scared, then the man looked scared."

"I'm not saying she made it up, Chief, I'm just
telling you that it certainly doesn't seem to fit Mr.
Franklin's personality, that's all," I told him, stifling a
sigh. "Anyway, what are you going to do about it?"

"I'm not going to do anything about it, but—"

"You've got to!" I said. "Mr. Franklin is a suspect
in this case, and if we lose him, then—"

"But I know the bus driver," Chief McGinnis
continued. "He's married to a cousin of mine, and he

said he'd call me if Mr. Franklin got off the bus before it reached San Antonio."

I could tell that Chief McGinnis was really enjoying having pulled a fast one on me, but I, in turn, acted as if I didn't realize what had happened. I'm sure that really bugged him. "Well, what'll happen once Mr. Franklin gets to San Antonio?" I asked.

"I called a friend of mine on the San Antonio police force," Chief McGinnis said. "He's going to arrange for one of his men to follow Mr. Franklin to wherever it is he's going."

"You sure do have a lot of police friends around the country," I said. "I'm impressed."

"I was one of the officers in the national police chiefs' organization a couple of years ago," Chief McGinnis said proudly. "I met a lot of people, and I made a lot of friends."

I knew this part of the conversation had to do with Chief McGinnis's wanting me to know that he isn't dumb, even though a lot of people in River Heights think he is. Just for the record, I've never thought he was dumb. I just think he's . . . well, he misses some of the more *important* details in investigations.

"I've always said that we're fortunate to have someone like you running the River Heights Police Department, Chief McGinnis," I said, continuing to butter him up. "Will you let me know if you hear anything from the bus driver?"

"Of course I will, Nancy," Chief McGinnis said. "All of the citizens of River Heights have to work together to keep our streets safe from criminals."

"That's true," I agreed. "And you know that you can always count on me. I have to run now. Thanks again for calling me with this update. Bye!" I quickly hung up the receiver.

I looked at my watch. If I didn't hurry, I'd be late for lunch with Lizzie and Janice Romer. I checked the address of Janice Romer's apartment, then headed out the front door.

I was glad that the traffic on River Street wasn't very heavy. Sometimes getting around during lunch hour can be difficult. In a short time I reached Janice's place, turned into the parking lot, found a space that I assumed was for visitors, and pulled into it. I quickly found Janice's apartment in one of the buildings at the rear and rang the bell.

Janice answered the door. "Oh, Nancy! Thank you so much for coming," she said.

She looked to me as though she might have been crying, because her eyes were a bit red. But then I realized it might have been allergies. On the way over to the apartment, I'd passed a sign at one of the town's allergy clinics that said the tree pollen was high today.

Just then Lizzie came up behind her and added, "We knew we could count on you, Nancy Drew."

"Of course," I said. "I'm glad you called! It was a nice surprise."

"Lunch is ready," Janice said. "The bathroom is just down the hall, if you want to freshen up."

"Thanks," I said.

When I got back, Lizzie and Janice were already seated at the small dining table.

"We're just having salads, but I made several kinds," Janice said, "so there should be something here that you'll like."

"Oh, this all looks wonderful," I said, sitting down at the only remaining chair. "You two are such great cooks. I'm envious!"

Within minutes I could tell that they were both very upset about something, but I tried to be as upbeat as possible while I helped myself to small portions of several of the salads. I took a couple of bites, then decided to cut to the chase. "Hannah said you sounded very upset, Lizzie. Why don't you tell me what's wrong?"

"Well, we're not exactly sure where to start," Janice said. She produced a letter, which she must have had on her lap. "I guess this is the best way. We wanted you to read this, and tell us what you make of it."

I wiped my hands on my napkin, then took the letter from her. It was from a lawyer in a town about twenty miles down the Muskoka River, but I wasn't familiar with his name. As I read the letter, I felt chills go up and down my spine. It informed the Romer sisters that a forensic linguist had determined that the handwritten *third* will, in which the late Albert Washington gave them a lot of money, was a fake, and that they were going to have to repay all the money they had received.

I looked up. Both Lizzie and Janice were staring at me expectantly.

"Well, this letter certainly *looks* genuine, but I've never heard of this law firm," I said. "Of course, that doesn't mean much. Dad knows a lot of lawyers in the state and across the entire country, and I've heard many of their names in conversation, but he certainly doesn't know all of them." I shook my head in disbelief. "Still, I can't believe this is really true."

"We're so upset, Nancy—as you can imagine," Lizzie said. "We still have some of the money left, but we don't have it all, and there's no way we could repay it."

"If we did, we'd be destitute again," Janice added. "We were just starting to get our lives together!"

I remembered when I first met Janice and Lizzie

Romer. They lived on a small farm several miles from River Heights. Their parents had died in an automobile accident, leaving them almost penniless. Still, they managed to survive by selling eggs and whatever vegetables they could raise. It was their kindness to Albert Washington that allowed them to have a life. They had no idea he was as wealthy as he was the day he stopped by their little farm and bought some of their fresh tomatoes. He stayed most of one afternoon, listening to the twins' life stories, and their secret for how they got more eggs from their chickens and how they made sure insects didn't destroy their tomato vines. He seemed to take a liking to the girls. After that afternoon, he would visit them a couple of times a week, just to chat. The three of them had become very close by the time he got ill and couldn't drive to their farm anymore.

When Mr. Washington invited Janice and Lizzie to his house, they were stunned by his wealth. They were also angered by the way that the Smalley family treated him. As his closest relatives, the Smalleys had told everyone they should be the ones to take care of him at his house, around the clock. But sometimes they left him alone for long periods of time. It was a good thing Janice and Lizzie got there when they did: Albert was lying on the floor, unable to get up! It was quite obvious to the Romer twins that the Smalleys were only interested in Albert Washington's money. And, in fact, the Smalleys soon began bragging to everyone that Albert Washington had written a second will, leaving his entire estate to them.

The Smalleys tried to keep the Romer twins from visiting Albert Washington, but the girls managed to visit when the Smalleys left him alone—which, toward the end of his life, was almost always. It was during one of these times, I was sure, that Albert Washington wrote out a third will—the one I found—which left a large portion of his fortune to Janice and Lizzie. The rest went to some other relatives who had been named in the *first* will, and had contested the second one that left everything to the Smalleys.

"We don't know what we're going to do, Nancy," Lizzie said. "We drove over to River City last night, near where we used to live, and talked to a police officer we know there."

"He said the letter looked genuine to him," Janice added, "although he also admitted he was no expert."

I folded up the letter and put it back inside the envelope. "May I take this and let my father look at it?" I said.

"Oh, would you do that for us?" Lizzie said. "We know we can trust you."

"I don't mind at all," I said.

124

We finished the rest of the delicious lunch, then I told Lizzie and Janice that I needed to leave, but that I would be in touch with them by tomorrow at the latest.

As I headed back toward my house, I was positive that the Smalleys were behind the letter Lizzie and Janice had received, and I had a hunch that they were somehow behind the problems I'd been having at the library as well. Maybe Deirdre was off the hook.

I had just turned onto my street, when I decided that I wanted Ned with me when I confronted the Smalley sisters about all this. I called his cell phone.

"Hey, Ned. Where are you?" I asked when he picked up.

"I'm parked in front of your house, ready to walk up to the door and ring the bell," Ned said. "Where are you?"

"I'm on my way back from lunch with the Romer sisters," I told him. "Stay where you are; I'm a second away. We have another stop to make."

"Okay," Ned said.

The next minute, I pulled up alongside Ned's car. He hopped out and got into mine.

"Where are we going?" Ned asked.

"To the Smalleys' house," I told him. I quickly filled him in on what Janice and Lizzie had told me.

"The Smalleys really are behind all this, Ned, I just know they are."

"Well, it's certainly all starting to fit together that way, Nancy," Ned agreed.

I listened as he reviewed all the things that had happened since the day the clock was stolen from the library, including all the things that had happened to me as chair of the decoration committee for the library anniversary celebration.

"Yes—now it's easy to see the Smalleys' hands in everything," I said. "Someone *really* angry with me is doing all these things—and I know they qualify."

Ned nodded.

Just then we turned onto the Smalleys' street and started past the front of their house. As we neared the sidewalk in front of their porch, I couldn't believe what I saw.

"What in the world is Ellis Lamsley doing here?" I gasped.

Ned didn't say anything. I think he was as confused as I was. "Maybe they have some library books that are overdue?" he said.

"Yeah, right," I said, smirking at his joke.

Ned was just being facetious. First, I'd never seen either of the Smalley girls reading for pleasure; they were usually shopping and socializing. Second, the library didn't send their staff out to collect overdue fines. Ellis could only be there on a personal matter. This whole mystery was getting more and more bizarre.

That's when I remembered the name. Ellis's last name. Lamsley.

Just as I turned a corner, my cell phone rang. Ned answered it for me; it was Bess. She wanted us to meet her and George at George's house.

"You timed your call just right," I said. "I have something really weird to tell you."

We were about five blocks from George's house, so it didn't take us long to get there.

Ned and I hurried to the front door and rang the bell.

I could tell by the look on George's face when she opened the door that something had happened—and it wasn't good.

"Break it to me gently, George," I said, as Ned and I went inside.

Bess was sitting in a chair with a frozen expression on her face. Suddenly I was scared. "Is it Dad or Hannah?" I managed to ask. "Has something happened to them?"

"Oh, no, nothing like that, Nancy," Bess said. She stood up. "It's still bad, though—and we wanted to be with you when you heard."

"Okay," I said, steeling myself. "I'm ready."

"All the posters that we made for the library celebration were ruined by leaking water," George said.

I just looked at her—half relieved, half angry. "What happened? Did the library flood or something?" I asked. I could just see some major water catastrophe devastating the library.

"No, the leak was just down in the basement, where you'd said in your note that we should store the posters," Bess said. "A water pipe leaked on them."

"I didn't tell anyone to store any posters in the basement," I said. "Someone else wrote that note." Everyone was just staring at me. I took a deep breath. "Well, I also have a surprise for you two," I told Bess and George. "Ned and I just saw Ellis Lamsley going into the Smalleys' house."

Bess gasped.

"You're kidding me!" George said. "Why would he be doing that?"

"That's what we're going to find out," I said. "I want the four of us to go to the library and see if we can find Ellis," I said. I looked each one of them straight in the eye. "After that, I'm going to resign from the library committee," I added emphatically.

12

What's in a Name?

The four of us piled into my car, and we headed for the Mahoney Library. When we got there, I couldn't find a parking space in front, so I drove around to the back.

"We can use the service entrance," I told everyone. "That'll be closer to Mrs. Corning's office. I won't have to face the rest of the librarians, who probably think I'm a total failure."

"You are not a failure, Nancy," Bess said. "Repeat after me: 'I am not a failure.'"

"I am not a failure," I repeated halfheartedly.

"Well, that'll certainly convince a lot of people," George said.

As we headed up the steps of the loading dock, I started rehearsing what I was going to say to Mrs.

129

he was going to pull a fast one on us. He launched into some of the most fantastic stories I had ever heard. I could tell that he was really enjoying suggesting that some of the most important citizens of River Heights might be criminals.

"Excuse me, Mr. Franklin, but I'm thirsty," I interrupted him. "Would you mind if I get a glass of water?"

"Oh, sure, sure. Just help yourself," Mr. Franklin said. With a nod of his head, he added, "The kitchen's that way."

I stood up and headed in the direction of the nod. I wasn't really thirsty—and even if I had been, there was no way that I would drink out of any glass I found in his cupboards. I had suddenly thought that if Mr. Franklin had stolen the library clock, he might not have sold it yet, and it could still be somewhere in his house.

Corning. But just as we opened the back door, I saw her to our immediate left. She was ripping up some of the posters, and they seemed pretty dry to me.

Bess and George gasped.

"You don't have permission to be back here!" Mrs. Corning screamed at us. "What's the meaning of this?"

"I think we need to ask you the same question, Mrs. Corning," Ned said. He looked at me. "Don't we, Nancy?"

Slowly all of the pieces of the puzzle were starting to fit together—and it wasn't the picture I had expected to see.

"I don't understand, Mrs. Corning," I finally said, my voice barely above a whisper. "I was trying so hard to make the library celebration a success."

Suddenly Mrs. Corning buried her face in her hands and started crying. "I wanted you to look foolish, Nancy," she said, sobbing. "Because . . . I blame you for Helen's leaving River Heights!"

I was stunned. I couldn't believe that Mrs. Corning had been harboring all this ill will toward me for so long—and only now, it came out!

I walked over and took her by the hand. "Why don't we discuss this someplace else?" I said as gently as I could.

Mrs. Corning looked unsure at first, but quickly

caved. "All right," she said, looking up at us with her tear-stained face. "There's an old table and some chairs on the other side of those packing boxes where we can sit. I just can't go back out into the main library now—now that you've found me. I can't face the other librarians."

As the five of us headed across the storeroom, I said, "There's really no reason for anyone else to know about this, Mrs. Corning. We can figure out a way to get everything back on track for the celebration."

Mrs. Corning started shaking her head. "No, no, it's too late for that, Nancy," she said.

We reached the table and chairs and all sat down.

"It's never too late for anything," I said, trying to sound conciliatory. "If you think about something long enough, you can always find a solution to any problem."

Mrs. Corning nodded.

"I knew how much Helen wanted to be an actress, so I suggested that she live with Mr. Corning, while she took acting lessons—to see how everything worked out," I said. "In retrospect, I should have been sensitive to your feelings, too—and I'm so sorry."

"I was being selfish, though. I was thinking only of myself," Mrs. Corning admitted. "Trying to make you look bad these past few days has been so hard for me; I'm ashamed about how I've acted, what I've done out of unreasonable resentment. Really, I should have just spoken to you about this before Helen left." She paused a moment, and looked at all of us with weepy eyes. "I plan to make a public apology for what I did to you, and then I will resign my position as head librarian."

"Well, wait—you did nothing illegal," I said. "I don't think your apology needs to leave this room." I just didn't have the heart to make this public. It might tarnish her professional reputation—and she'd been so good to the library. I turned to everyone else. "What do you think?"

They all nodded, but I could tell that they weren't too happy with letting Mrs. Corning get away with what she had done to me.

"I suppose, for the celebration, we could always make a papier-mâché replica of the library clock," Bess suggested. She looked at George and Ned. "Together we can all make sure this is a happy occasion, can't we?"

"Sure, Bess," Ned agreed. "Just like Nancy said, if you think long and hard enough about something, you can always figure out a solution."

"Mrs. Corning?" a voice called from the door leading to the main library.

"It's Chief McGinnis," I whispered. "I wonder what he wants."

"Are you in there, Mrs. Corning?" Chief McGinnis called again.

"Yes, yes, we're back here, just talking about the library celebration, Chief," Mrs. Corning said in as composed a voice as she could manage. "What was it you needed?"

When Chief McGinnis saw all of us, he said, "I actually wanted to ask you a question about one of your librarians, Mrs. Corning. But I'm glad that Nancy is here, because she needs to hear this too."

Mrs. Corning looked puzzled. "I don't understand," she said. "Is something wrong?"

"That's what I want to find out," Chief McGinnis said.

"Which librarian are you talking about?" I asked.

"Ellis Lamsley," Chief McGinnis said.

I shot my friends a quick glance. Incredibly, I had almost forgotten the reason we had come to the library in the first place.

"We got a court order to examine Mr. Franklin's bank account, and we found something very interesting," Chief McGinnis continued.

"Really?" I said. "What?"

"Mr. Franklin deposited a couple of checks from Ellis Lamsley into his account," the chief said. "The first one was for two hundred dollars, and the second one was for four hundred dollars."

"Why was Ellis giving Mr. Franklin money?" George asked.

"I don't have any idea," Chief McGinnis said.

"Maybe it was a loan," Bess said. "Maybe he felt sorry for Mr. Franklin."

"I don't think that was it at all," I said. "I think it was blackmail."

"*Blackmail?*" everyone cried.

"Why would Mr. Franklin be blackmailing Ellis?" Ned asked.

Just as I started to explain, another voice said, "Well, I didn't know we were having a committee meeting this morning!"

We all turned and saw Ellis standing just a few feet away. I had no idea how long he had been there or how much he'd heard of what we were saying, but I decided to find out.

"Where are the jewels, Ellis?" I asked.

Everyone turned to stare at me, and probably didn't see Ellis turn pale.

"What jewels?" Ellis asked.

"You know what jewels I'm talking about," I continued. "The jewels you dug up after you stole the library clock."

Ellis turned to run, but Ned was too fast for him. He got up and tackled Ellis before he reached the door to the main library.

Ellis landed with a thud and cried out in pain. "I think you broke my arm, you thug!" he whined.

"I thought you were an athlete, Ellis," George said. "Turns out you're nothing but a wimp."

"Ellis Lamsley, you're under arrest," Chief McGinnis said. He read Ellis his rights while he was putting handcuffs on him.

"My name's not Lamsley," Ellis said. He turned to me and spat out his next words. "It's *Smalley*. Even the great Nancy Drew didn't realize that 'Lamsley' is an anagram for 'Smalley,'" he said, sneering.

I didn't see the point of telling Ellis that, from the beginning, I had been curious about his last name, so I just kept quiet.

Chief McGinnis started to lead Ellis away, but Ellis said, "Don't you want to hear the rest of the story?"

"Of course," I said, "but in the movies this is usually where someone says that you shouldn't say anything without your lawyer present," I said.

"My lawyer *is* present," Ellis said. "You're looking at him!"

"Oh, *please!*" Bess said, and rolled her eyes.

"I'm smarter than any lawyer in this town," Ellis said. "No jury in River Heights will convict me after they hear my side of the story."

It suddenly occurred to me that Ellis was a smooth enough talker that he might be right—but I really did have more faith in a River Heights jury to find him guilty than he did.

"Come on," Chief McGinnis said.

He grabbed Ellis by the shoulder, but Ellis pulled free and faced me defiantly. For just a split second I wondered if he'd try to attack me, just to get even in some way, but he didn't move. He did tell us all what happened, though, and Chief McGinnis let him.

The Smalleys had promised Ellis, their cousin, that they would send him to the university to become a librarian, but when I discovered Albert Washington's last will, which disinherited the Smalleys, they couldn't afford to keep their promise. Ellis had to work in fast-food restaurants to pay his tuition. From the way he described this, it was easy to tell that he thought he was above that sort of thing. His anger toward me kept building, and he promised himself that one day he would get even with me—and return the money to his family.

When Ellis learned that Ben Mullins had given all of his papers, drawings, and materials to the Mahoney Library, he used his charm to get this job, so he could have full access to the documents. He had always believed the story about the buried jewels, and after reading all of the jeweler's documents, he was positive that the clue to where they were buried was in the library clock.

He had the plan all worked out. Unfortunately he didn't realize that Mr. Franklin had come back to the library unexpectedly, to get some tools he needed. He saw Ellis taking the clock out of the wall. Franklin told Ellis he'd have to give him some money to keep quiet about the theft. Ellis figured that he could afford to give Mr. Franklin a little cash, considering what he'd be able to sell the jewels for. He didn't really expect Mr. Franklin to get as greedy as he did; he decided he wanted some of the jewels for himself. That's when the Smalleys—who knew about Ellis's strategy—decided they had had enough. The entire clan, including Ellis, went to Franklin's house and threatened to put him someplace where no one would ever find him.

"Mr. Franklin left the next day for Texas," Ellis said. He gave a big laugh. "We would have kept our promise too—and he knew it."

"So, Ralph Mullins and his family had nothing to do with any of this?" I asked.

Ellis shook his head violently. "No!" he shouted. "And they don't deserve the jewels, either."

"Did you make the telephone call from Henry Mead, and send the letter to the Romer sisters?" I asked.

Ellis nodded. "A little harsh, yes. But I wanted you to be totally confused," he said.

Chief McGinnis grabbed Ellis by the arm. "We've heard enough," he said. He radioed his officer who was in the patrol car outside. "I'm bringing a perpetrator out," he added. "I've solved the mystery of the library clock."

George and Bess looked at me and rolled their eyes.

Just then Deirdre walked in. "What is going on here?" she demanded. She turned to me. "Nancy, do you have any idea how little time there is until the library celebration? You've really not shown any leadership at all in this, and frankly, I think that—"

"Deirdre," George said. "Stuff it!"

Deirdre blinked. "Nobody talks to me that way!" she said, glaring. She took a deep breath and let it out. "That does it. I'm taking myself off this committee! I will not be a part of anything that's going to fail, and fail miserably."

"Oh, thank you, Deirdre," I said. "I just hate to fire people—and now you've saved me that task."

For a minute I thought Deirdre was going to explode. But instead she just wheeled around and stormed out of the library.

"I have a feeling that this committee will get twice as much work done now," Ned said.

"So do I," I agreed.

* * * *

Ellis had the library clock hidden in his apartment. He had taken it apart, so he could get to an engraving inside. At first it looked like the fabled map to the jewels. On closer inspection, though, it appeared to be a map of River Heights. Ellis didn't have any jewels in his possession, and later admitted to not finding the map. Where, then, was the map to the jewels? Did it exist? That was a mystery for another day!

Chief McGinnis returned the clock to the library, and Ned headed a crew of townspeople who lovingly reassembled and reinstalled it. If anything, I thought the clock looked better than ever.

Over the next few weeks we worked feverishly to get everything ready for the library anniversary celebration. We made it, and the party was anything but usual.

"I have a pretty big role in *Mystery Depot* this fall," Helen Corning whispered to me. She'd flown in the day before for the celebration. "You'll never believe who my love interest is." She whispered the name of a man who used to be big in movies, but now was seen only on television. "Don't tell, though, because he hasn't signed his contract yet!"

"Oh, I won't tell—but it sounds great!" I told her.

"I know," Helen said. She gave me a big hug. "Thanks for suggesting that I move to California."

I was sure that her mother hadn't said anything at all about what had happened in the library, so I certainly wasn't going to either.

Just then someone tapped a spoon on a glass, and we all turned to see who it was. Mrs. Mahoney was standing underneath the library clock. "I have an announcement to make," she said. She motioned for Mrs. Corning and Helen to join her. "Mrs. Corning is resigning her position as head librarian of the Mahoney Library, effective immediately, and she's going to California with her daughter, Helen. Let's show our appreciation for all that she's done."

That brought forth some heartfelt applause from the crowd. I was just so glad that things had worked out. I was sure Mrs. Corning would have resigned anyway, because of what she had done. But this way, it almost didn't matter.

After the toast, Ned, Bess, George, and I circulated throughout the library, taking in all of the compliments for the displays, but especially for the library clock.

Then, as the crowds began to thin, the four of us found ourselves standing underneath the clock, looking up at it, almost reverently.

"I wonder what this clock will see over the next few years," I said.

"There's no telling," George said.

"Well, whatever it is, I guess we'll start finding out tomorrow," a voice behind us said.

We all turned and saw Evaline Waters with a big grin on her face.

"What do you mean, Ms. Waters?" Bess asked.

"Mrs. Mahoney has asked me to be the head librarian, at least temporarily," Ms. Waters said. "Since the library is now short *two* librarians, I told her I would."

"Oh, it'll be just like old times," I said. I gave Ms. Waters a big hug.

"I'll need some help, though," Ms. Water said. "I was sort of counting on all four of you."

"Oh, we'll be glad to do whatever you need us to do," Bess said.

"Right," I agreed. "After all, we need somebody to guard the library clock to make sure nothing like this ever happens again."

REDISCOVER THE CLASSIC MYSTERIES OF NANCY DREW

$5.99 ($8.99 CAN) each
AVAILABLE AT YOUR LOCAL BOOKSTORE OR LIBRARY

Grosset & Dunlap • A division of Penguin Young Readers Group
A member of Penguin Group (USA), Inc. • A Pearson Company
www.penguin.com/youngreaders

HAVE YOU READ ALL OF THE ALICE BOOKS?

PHYLLIS REYNOLDS NAYLOR

STARTING WITH ALICE
Atheneum Books for
 Young Readers
 0-689-84395-X
Aladdin Paperbacks
 0-689-84396-8

ALICE IN BLUNDERLAND
Atheneum Books for
 Young Readers
 0-689-84397-6

LOVINGLY ALICE
Atheneum Books for
 Young Readers
 0-689-84399-2

THE AGONY OF ALICE
Atheneum Books for
 Young Readers
 0-689-31143-5
Aladdin Paperbacks
 0-689-81672-3

ALICE IN RAPTURE,
 SORT-OF
Atheneum Books for
 Young Readers
 0-689-31466-3
Aladdin Paperbacks
 0-689-81687-1

RELUCTANTLY ALICE
Atheneum Books for
 Young Readers
 0-689-31681-X
Aladdin Paperbacks
 0-689-81688-X

ALL BUT ALICE
Atheneum Books for
 Young Readers
 0-689-31773-5
Aladdin Paperbacks
 0-689-85044-1

ALICE IN APRIL
Atheneum Books for
 Young Readers
 0-689-31805-7
Aladdin Paperbacks
 0-689-81686-3

ALICE IN-BETWEEN
Atheneum Books for
 Young Readers
 0-689-31890-0
Aladdin Paperbacks
 0-689-81685-5

ALICE THE BRAVE
Atheneum Books for
 Young Readers
 0-689-80095-9
Aladdin Paperbacks
 0-689-80598-5

ALICE IN LACE
Atheneum Books for
 Young Readers
 0-689-80358-3
Aladdin Paperbacks
 0-689-80597-7

OUTRAGEOUSLY ALICE
Atheneum Books for
 Young Readers
 0-689-80354-0
Aladdin Paperbacks
 0-689-80596-9

ACHINGLY ALICE
Atheneum Books for
 Young Readers
 0-689-80533-9
Aladdin Paperbacks
 0-689-80595-0
Simon Pulse
 0-689-86396-9

ALICE ON THE OUTSIDE
Atheneum Books for
 Young Readers
 0-689-80359-1
Simon Pulse
 0-689-80594-2

GROOMING OF ALICE
Atheneum Books for
 Young Readers
 0-689-82633-8
Simon Pulse
 0-689-84618-5

ALICE ALONE
Atheneum Books for
 Young Readers
 0-689-82634-6
Simon Pulse
 0-689-85189-8

SIMPLY ALICE
Atheneum Books for
 Young Readers
 0-689-84751-3
Simon Pulse
 0-689-85965-1

PATIENTLY ALICE
Atheneum Books for
 Young Readers
 0-689-82636-2
Simon Pulse
 0-689-87073-6

INCLUDING ALICE
Atheneum Books for
 Young Readers
 0-689-82637-0

CASTAWAYS

Think it would be fun to get stuck on a deserted island with the guy you sort of like? Well, try adding the girl who gets on your nerves big-time (*and* who's crushing on the same guy), the bossiest kid in school, your annoying little brother, and a bunch of other people, all of whom have their own ideas about how things should be done. Oh, and have I mentioned that there's no way off this island, and no one knows where you are?

Still sound great? Didn't think so.

Now all I have to worry about is getting elected island leader, finding something to wear for a dance (if you can believe that), and surviving a hurricane, all while keeping my crush away from Little Miss Priss. Oh, and one other teeny-tiny little thing: surviving.

Get me outta here!

Read all the books in the Castaways trilogy:

#1 Worst Class Trip Ever

#2 Weather's Here, Wish You Were Great

#3 Isle Be Seeing You

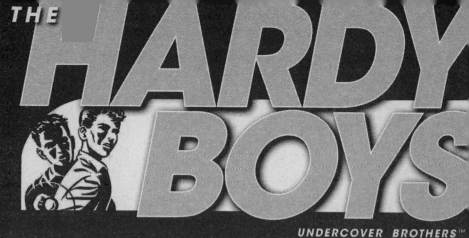

THE HARDY BOYS

UNDERCOVER BROTHERS™

They've got motorcycles,
their cases are ripped from the headlines,
and they work for ATAC:
American Teens Against Crime.

CRIMINALS, BEWARE:

THE HARDY BOYS ARE ON YOUR TRAIL!

Starting in **Summer 2005**,
Frank and Joe will begin telling all-new stories of crime,
danger, death-defying stunts, mystery, and teamwork.

Ready? Set? Fire it up!